# THE
# READER

## M.K. HARKINS

# DEDICATION

## Nancy Bailey

### MAY 6TH, 1953 - MARCH 29TH, 2013

*You are loved, and not forgotten.*

*An angel on earth, but I think heaven needed you.*

*All I have to do is remember your smile*

*and I feel better.*

*Until we meet again . . .*

# BOOKS BY M.K. HARKINS

### Intentional:

*Intentional is a real page turner which got me more and more involved. It developed into an intense situation which developed into another and then exploded into a great climax!*

~Amazon Reviewer

*This book is a great read. It is very well written and I would recommend it to anyone who is interested in intense romance novels with a little bit of suspense in the process*

~My eBook Café

*Have you ever read a book and once you are finished you want to seek out the highest mountain to shout to the world "READ THIS BOOK?"*

~ Lola Kay

# Books by M.K. Harkins

### Unintentional:

*I have to say in all honesty. . . . I LOVED this book!!!!! I actually liked it even more then Intentional. I thought this book flowed very well and I loved how she switched off the POV's during the chapters. I felt we got the full feeling of the story that way. This book is listed as a standalone and I truly believe it can be read as one. The author does a wonderful job of recapping the end of Intentional from Cade's POV , that you really don't miss anything from the first book.*

~ Jennifer from Book Bitches Blog

*This story is great. I love how the author gave me a love story with some mystery thrown into it. This is one of those books that you don't want to put down until you've finished it, because you have to know what happens next. So in this book you have a great story, awesome characters, excellent writing, and a happy reader at the end. I highly recommend this book*

~ Leigh Broxton

# BOOKS BY M.K. HARKINS

### *Breaking Braydon:*

*I was left in complete awe after finishing this unbelievably heart-felt book. M. K. Harkins has stolen my heart, and I honestly don't want it back. This story left me wanting so much more and yet feeling completely content and satisfied. Watching these amazing characters love and support each other was beyond description at times at how it made my heart swell with pride and admiration. What a magnificent journey I was given the privilege to watch and take part in, and I will forever remember the story that made me cry tears of joy and rapture*

~ Shadowplay (Amazon Reviewer)

*I loved this book! It's hopeful and uplifting, emotional without being overwrought. And the author has made incredible, jaw-dropping strides in her craft. The writing is clean, the plot swift, the characters engaging, and the dialogue snappy and often quite funny. Even the secondary characters have heart and humor, and it's my great hope the author will spin-off a story or two for each of them.*

*If you enjoy inspiring, witty romance with an upbeat, playful vibe, Breaking Braydon is for you. It's the perfect way to spend the day, curled up with Braydon and Jain*

~ Story Girl

# BOOKS BY M.K. HARKINS

### *Taking Tiffany*

*This story has a lot of romance, adventure, mystery, intrigue, and surprises, one after the other. Just when you think you have it figured out it goes in a different way. It was a very entertaining read and I definitely recommend it. Of course, it has a HEA.*

~ \*\*Amazon Top 1000 Reviewer

*This has quickly bumped up my favorite books list. I really loved it. Loved it so much, as soon as I finished, I went right back to the beginning to read it again!*

*I highly recommend. Lovable characters, surprising plot twists and smoldering chemistry all make Taking Tiffany a must read.*

~ More Than A Review

*Sweet with just enough mystery. I never would've guessed the outcome which was amazing. At the same time it was touching and adorable which made it the perfect romantic book. There's just enough romance and just enough mystery/suspense.*

~ Amazon Reviewer

# CHAPTER 1

*I* *AM DEAD.*

My eyes cracked open for a moment before I squeezed them shut again. The blazing sunlight ratcheted up my headache from dull to code red. Maybe not dead—not quite yet. I lay on my stomach with my cheek pressed against the sand on a dark, gritty shore.

Waves lapped at my feet, making my one remaining tennis shoe feel tight and cold; I couldn't feel my other foot. I tried to spit some sand out of my mouth, but failed. The granules remained stuck to my tongue; weakness won.

No, not dead. I just wished I was.

"Look, Maddie!" said a young voice, maybe nine or ten years old. "A dead body!"

That would be me. Except, I wasn't quite there yet.

"Cool! I've never seen one before. Should we kick it?"

*That would not be helpful.* I braced myself, waiting for the inevitable pain that would soon follow. I groaned and tried to turn on my side.

"It's a zombie! Run!"

Sand sprayed in my face as the kids scrambled away. At least, now it was quiet. The only sound was the gentle lapping of the water on the shore. My head ached, my body was wet and freezing, and something warm oozed from my right shoulder. Not good.

What happened?

I searched, trying to remove the internal block, but came up empty. Almost as if an eraser had wiped all the words from a chalkboard, my mind a blur of colored dust.

I don't remember. Not one thing.

A wrenching pain clamped around my chest with an aching darkness so intense, I could barely breathe. Tears stung, and my heart slowed. Everything stilled. I focused on calming myself, working through the devastating emotional response brought with that one question—*what happened?*

"We've done our bit; just toss her on the shore." An old man rasped out the words like crackled paper.

A recent memory, I was sure.

"She could die if we leave her. She's lost a lot of blood," a younger male voice had said.

"It doesn't matter. We were paid to deliver her here. It's only a couple feet deep. Now give her a shove, and let's get going," said the old man.

"Sorry," the younger man had whispered in my ear.

That was the last thing I remembered before hearing the delinquent children contemplating my zombie demise. Blankness stretched before me, a darkness I couldn't penetrate.

With another groan, I lifted myself up into a sitting position and scanned the beach and surrounding area. I might not know who those men were or why I was dumped here, but I wasn't going to wait around to find out. A copse of trees and bushes was close, maybe thirty yards away, a suitable place to conceal myself and form a plan.

I took a quick inventory. Torn shirt, jeans with a hole in the left leg, and a missing shoe. Blood seeped from my upper arm. I moved back a little of the fabric, and a small round hole was the cause. The opening appeared jagged—a bullet hole? It was throbbing, but no pain—yet. Sweat formed above my brow. I leaned over to rest my head onto my bent knees.

"I think it's her," a deep, male voice said from about two feet away.

Great. I hadn't moved fast enough. My window to hide—gone.

"It looks like she might be hurt. Should we call for help?" another male voice asked.

"No! No calls. Either the Jacks or the police will find her."

I rubbed my temples. The police?

"Let's get her back to the compound and have Doc take a look at her," the first male voice commanded, sounding irritated.

Compound. That didn't sound good.

Time to take a look. I raised my head and squinted against the bright sunshine. Two men, around my age, stood looking down at me with hands on hips and furrowed brows.

"Who are you?" I asked in a whisper.

"Friends," the blond one answered. I blinked a few times,

trying to clear my vision. The sun glowed around his sweet and innocent face, the effect halo-like.

Maybe I died after all.

He sat next to me and touched my hand. Nope, he was real. Inquisitive green eyes and a warm smile lined his face. I should be freaked out, but a sense of comfort replaced my anxiety.

"Do I know you?" I asked.

"Not yet," answered the angelic one.

Oh. I waited for the fear to return, but calmness remained.

"We have to get going," the other man said, ignoring my question. I glanced in his direction. Every bit as handsome, but he was dark everywhere his friend was light. Dark hair, dark eyes, and a dark expression. He didn't look friendly—at all. A shiver traveled down my spine.

*Two men. One can be trusted, the other not.*

Was this a memory? Or was I jumping to conclusions?

The blond man said in a soothing voice, "We're going to help you. But we need to move you right away."

"No. I'm not going with you. I don't know you. I have to go..." Quick, I needed an excuse. Clearing my throat, I added, "I have to go to my Aunt Em's. She's expecting me."

"Good one. Yeah, the tornado that brings you to Oz is a bitch." A good-humored grin spread across the blond's face.

Apparently, I needed some practice lying. "Still not going." I put my head back onto my knees.

The dark-haired man, with his black, accusing eyes, squatted down next to me. "If we wanted to do you harm, don't you think we would've done so by now? This beach is deserted. We could've just given you a little push back into the water and waited."

If I had the energy to roll my eyes, I would. "Is that supposed to make me feel better?"

The blond one gave the other a punch in the arm. "You're going to scare her." He turned back to me. "That's Devon, my cousin. You don't have to worry about him. He's always a little intense."

I nodded. "Okaaay . . ."

"Oh, and my name is Archer. I'm the nice one."

Devon narrowed his eyes and shot Archer a menacing glare. "Can you stop with the chit-chat? This isn't the time or place. She's in danger. We need to get her out of here." He reached down to help me up, but stopped when he noticed my arm. "She's been shot. Archer, grab my backpack and the blanket from the back seat. We need to keep her warm and start first aid."

Archer turned and jogged to the same crop of trees where I had planned to escape. My strategy had been doomed from the start.

Devon looked back at me. His dark-lashed, smoky eyes pierced mine as if he were waiting for something.

"What?" I asked.

"I can't hear you."

"I didn't say anything."

He continued to stare. What was with this guy?

Archer returned, plunking down Devon's backpack, and placed the blanket over my legs. The chill lessened a bit. He unzipped the main compartment and pulled a first aid kit and a bottle of water.

My tongue swiped against my dry lips, and I almost lunged

for it.

Archer squatted next to me. "Do you need help?"

"No, I'm okay."

"Here." He handed it to me. "It'll help your headache."

"How did—"

"You've been wincing and rubbing your temples," Archer said.

Explosions rang through the quiet beach. The backpack split, and pieces of fabric scattered in every direction.

"Gunshots! Go, go go!" Devon yelled.

No way. "What?" I gasped and covered my ears.

"No time," Archer said as he slipped a hand under my legs and back and picked me up. He carried me, making a dash for the tree line. I looked over my shoulder and saw Devon duck as he grabbed the backpack following close behind.

"Ouch, ouch, ouch." The numbness left, replaced by a staggering pain in my shoulder. If the bullets didn't kill me, the rubbing and bouncing against Archer's chest with my injured arm would.

"Sorry," Archer whispered.

"What's happening?" I could barely get the words out with Archer jostling me over the uneven terrain.

"We'll get you to safety in a minute," Archer answered. After a chirping sound and a click, he opened the door, dropped me in the back seat, and hopped in next to me.

"Get in, now!" Archer yelled at Devon.

Devon jumped behind the wheel. "Hang on." He started the Jeep and tore out of the trees and onto a main highway. "We'll drive to the far side of the island, get her fixed up, and catch the next ferry."

"What about the Jacks? They'll be waiting for us at the dock." Archer's eyebrows drew together.

"They won't try anything in a public place. We'll lose them in Seattle," Devon answered, and the Jeep lurched forward.

"Okay. We'll do our usual." Archer turned to look out the back window.

With my heart about to beat out of my chest, I asked, "Were those gunshots meant for me? Who are these Jacks you keep talking about? Shouldn't we be calling the police?"

The men shot each other a glance through the rear view mirror.

Archer asked, "How much do you remember?"

Don't try to remember yet.

Ugh! Where did that annoying inner voice come from? I must be crazy, because that voice didn't belong to me.

"Nothing. I remember nothing." Tears threatened. I blinked to hold them back.

He took my hand and held it in his. I started to pull back, but he tightened his grip.

"Let go of—"

His eyes widened a bit, and he glanced at Devon. "I don't hear anything."

"I think she's blocking."

"What are you talking about?" I asked, finally yanking my hand free.

"Never mind. We don't have time to explain. We need to get you out of here." Devon said.

"Why? Who's after me? Did I do something wrong?" I

asked.

"Yes and no," Devon answered with a worried glance at me in the mirror. His eyes carefully swept the surrounding area before he turned off onto a deserted road and pulled over. "We really need to bandage your arm. Come on, let's make this quick.

"Who was shooting at us?"

Devon groaned. "We can talk about this at the compound. Right now, your health and safety are all we care about."

Archer hopped out of the Jeep and laid a blanket on the ground. He motioned me to come and sit.

I sat and Devon stood next to me, on guard.

More questions spun through my brain. "Would I be in jail in your compound?"

"No," Devon answered.

Archer sat next to me. "It'll be okay."

Not feeling like it was okay, I rubbed my forehead. "I have more questions."

"All right," Archer said. "Ask me anything."

Devon's eyes turned toward the sky, his lips moving in a silent dialogue. I'd guess he was either counting or swearing.

"Where is the compound, and why do you call it that?"

"It's in North Bend, you know, right before you get to the mountain pass," Archer said.

My mind drew a blank. "I don't know where that is."

"These questions could go on all day. I need to cover your wound." Devon leaned over to rip open the first aid kit, and pulled out the supplies—gauze, scissors, and some anti-bacterial cleanser. "I'll bandage your arm, then you can drill us with questions later."

"But—"

"Hold still." Devon placed his hand on my shoulder and began to cut my shirt. Where he touched, felt warm and tingly. My headache faded, and the tingly feeling moved and swirled around my entire body. I felt almost normal, the pain gone.

"Why does that feel so good?" I asked.

They both froze. Oh dear God, I said that out loud. Where did my filter go? The warmth started at my neck and worked its way up to the top of my head.

Archer, wide-eyed, shoved Devon to the side. "Don't you dare!"

"I didn't do anything! She's just feeling a little better." He glanced at me and asked, "Right?

"Yes. Um, yeah. Much better. I'm a little light-headed though."

Archer hesitated and studied Devon for a moment. "I'd better clean her up—just in case."

Devon raised his hands and said, "She's all yours."

Were these two always so competitive?

Archer finished applying the bandage with care. He held out his hand to help me up.

Would I feel the tingles with him, too? I slowly raised my good arm, and he seized my hand. Oh, good. It felt normal.

Although I'd begun to feel better physically, my emotional state was in question. Was I really considering going with them? My choices were limited. I could stay on the beach and dodge gunfire or go back to their compound. Confused and disorientated, I weighed my options. I shouldn't go with them. But the answer *yes* started to creep into my consciousness.

Did I trust them because they were so beautiful? Ugh. I hoped I wasn't that superficial. No, they saved me from whoever was shooting at us.

"We have some information about you. We've been sent to help you." Devon paused and looked at Archer.

"You seem to know more about me than I do."

"We think you're a Reader," Archer blurted.

"Oh, God. Now you're going to have to explain that," Devon said. "Can we just leave before the Jacks find us again? Come on, let's get her back into the Jeep."

I ignored him and closed my eyes for a moment. Reader. That word sparked something in me. I visualized thousands and thousands of books. They were lined up on shelves that took up an entire room—floor to ceiling. The room was safe and warm and beautiful. The memory filled me with a love so intense, it knocked the air from my lungs.

With a shaky breath, I said, "Yes! I read! I remember. Oh, thank goodness. I remembered something." And then it hit me.

*No!*

"You've done it now, Archer. She's going to remember before we get her to the doctor. We'll need to use a sedative."

"Why would I need a—" I started.

*Two kind, loving faces smiling at me.* My mom and dad. Then the picture vanished like a metal door had slammed shut. I held my head and tried to get the memory back, but it was gone.

For some reason, the image filled me with relief and sadness at the same time. A lump formed in my throat, and tears welled. "I think I remember my parents." I fought the urge to cry, and asked, "Why can't I remember?" Despite my best efforts, a few tears and a sob escaped.

"Hush," Archer said. "It's going to be all right." He helped me up and looped an arm around my waist.

*Get it together*. I let him lead me to their Jeep. Once Archer buckled me into the back seat, I calmed down a little. But the tears wouldn't stop.

Devon got back behind the steering wheel and rattled off instructions. "Make sure she changes out of her bloody shirt. I have an extra sweatshirt in the backpack. When we get to the ferry, put a pillow under her head, and she can pretend she's taking a nap. Call your dad, tell him we found her and to get Doc ready. Gunshot wound, possible hypothermia and shock. Oh, and get that blanket back on her."

Distracted by his demands, my crying tapered off. Man, he was bossy.

Archer gave a little waggle of his eyebrows. "We better do as he says or else he'll get grumpy."

"You mean *grumpier*? Is that possible?" I asked.

"Yeah." He rubbed my uninjured arm. "You're going to be all right."

Drying my face with my sleeve, I made a decision. I wouldn't succumb to the tears or the sadness that tried to burrow deep. Somewhere, somehow, I knew I was stronger than this.

"What are you waiting for? Let's get going," I called to the front seat.

Devon turned and looked back at me with narrowed eyes. Oh, now *he* was suspicious?

"The sooner we get to your compound, or whatever you call it, the quicker I can regain my memory and get back home."

His eyes softened. Wait. He wasn't the nice one. This couldn't be good.

"I do have a home to go to, right?" I asked.

"Yes," he answered. "You do have a home." He started the Jeep and reversed out of the trees.

I had a sinking feeling his idea of home and mine wouldn't be the same.

# CHAPTER 2

THE JOURNEY FROM THE San Juan Islands to North Bend, Washington passed without incident. Devon announced at the beginning of our trip there would be no more conversation until we arrived at the compound. After drinking water and warming up, I felt well enough to start in with my questions, but they both remained tight-lipped. Even the affable Archer, who looked like it took every bit of restraint not to respond, kept his mouth shut due to threats from Devon to report Archer to his dad.

*Devon is a jerk.*

We pulled up to a huge, gated community locked behind twelve-foot-high concrete walls and a wrought-iron gate. I peered between the black, metal pickets and spotted a few beige and brown homes sitting on large, ornately landscaped lots.

"So, is your dad the leader of your tribe?" I asked Archer.

"Kind of," he said.

"Has the question ban been lifted?" I asked.

"No." Devon's irritated voice grumbled from the front seat.

Archer gave my arm a pat. "We're almost there."

"This looks like a normal neighborhood," I said.

"We're back," Devon shouted to the gatehouse guard. Dressed in a blue military uniform, the stocky male sentry wore a rifle slung over his shoulder.

"I take it back. This is not normal."

"The guard is here for us. It's important we have privacy." Archer unrolled his window and flashed some sort of badge.

I examined the towering walls surrounding the neighborhood. The sun was bright, reflecting off a wire sitting two inches above the wall as far as the eye could see.

Hmm. I'd bet that wire would not be fun to touch. Maybe even deadly?

"Why do you need this much privacy?" I rubbed my sweaty hands down the legs of my tattered jeans.

"All in good time, my pretty." Archer's eyes crinkled at the corners.

I groaned. "That again? You plan to use that against me for the duration of my stay here?"

Archer burst out laughing. "You gotta admit—that was lame. Auntie Em's? Who doesn't know that line?"

Even though the crying portion of my ordeal was over, I didn't laugh along.

My shoulders sagged. "I don't know. I'm a little confused."

"Oh, that's right. Sorry." He rubbed the back of his neck and his eyes gentled when he met my distressed expression.

"It's okay."

He leaned in and with lips close to my ear, he said, "Don't worry about anything. I'll make sure nothing bad happens to you while you're with us. If anyone bothers you, just come to me. Okay?"

"What are you two whispering about back there?" Devon asked.

He was bossy *and* nosy.

"I was just telling her about the hiking paths around here." Archer smiled and winked.

"There won't be any hiking for a while. You got that, Archer?"

"Got it," Archer answered back with crossed arms and a frown.

This was the second time I sensed tension between them. I tried to diffuse it by saying, "I probably won't feel like hiking for at least a few days." I turned back toward Archer. "We could go then?"

"No," Devon's clipped voice answered for him.

Archer shrugged. "He's right. We'll probably need to get you through the initiation first."

"What initiation?" I asked, but wasn't sure I wanted to know. Crawling into a soft bed and sleeping for days or weeks sounded like a good plan.

"We'll get to all that after Doc sees you," Devon said, giving me a brief glance in the mirror.

I leaned back in my seat and decided to accept my fate . . . for now. After we passed through the guard station, we crisscrossed through the peaceful neighborhood with its wrought iron fences, large yards and expensive homes.

The unique architecture elevated the neighborhood from

generic to eclectic, a mix of Frank Lloyd Wright with a little Le Corbusier thrown in. Contemporary lines, huge window walls, simple millwork with clean, straight lines.

I could remember particular architects and their individual styles, but nothing about myself? That didn't seem right.

Even with my lack of memory, though, there was something about Archer and Devon that brought me a sense of comfort, maybe even belonging. It was almost like I knew them before. But no, I was sure they would have mentioned it.

"Who owns all these houses?" I asked.

"We all do," Devon said.

"Really? How many people live here?" I turned toward Archer.

"Three hundred and forty-two," Devon answered, even though I'd spoken to Archer.

"Hey, you got a little information from the Grinch." Archer chuckled.

I giggled into my hand, not wanting Devon to shut down the flow of information again.

The neighborhood was quiet as we continued to weave our way through the twisty streets. "It doesn't look like anyone's home."

Wait. Something was off. I hadn't noticed it at first, but the shades were drawn in every single house. There weren't garbage cans out at the curb; no bikes or toys littered the lawns. The neighborhood seemed quiet. Too clean and perfect.

"People don't live in these houses, do they?" I asked.

"Perceptive," Devon said under his breath.

"I heard that." I curbed the desire to stick out my tongue, opting for restraint. Instead, I kept up with my questions.

"Why are they empty?"

"It's the privacy issue I mentioned before," Archer said.

"You need empty houses in order to maintain privacy? These homes had to cost a fortune. How did your compound people pay for this?" I glanced back and forth between them.

Devon brushed his fingers through his unruly hair, making it even messier, and let out a long breath.

"Well?" I asked, trying to keep my voice sweet to coax out the answer.

"I know you're curious, but we won't be able to answer all your questions right away," Devon said.

"Why?"

He slowed the car and turned to look at me with a raised eyebrow.

"Another question. Gotcha." I bit my lip and decided to busy myself by looking out the back window, memorizing the path we'd taken. Maybe I'd need the information one day.

The last leg of our journey led us down a bumpy, dirt road with a large mountain looming in front of us.

The car came to a halt. "We're here," Archer said as he unbuckled his seat belt.

"Deploy the signal," Devon instructed Archer.

Archer jumped out of the car and bent over a small tree stump. He reached inside, pulled out a metal bar, and twisted. With a push downward, it disappeared back into the ground.

"What did he just do?"

Devon tapped his fingers on the wheel. "You can't help yourself, can you?"

"You don't have to be so . . . so, I don't know, *bratty* about it." I threw my good hand up in frustration.

A smile tugged on his lips. He coughed into his hand.

*I saw you smile.*

Archer hopped back into the seat next to me. "All set."

Devon reached over to the glovebox and removed a small, rectangular instrument, pressing lighted buttons at a rapid speed. What now?

A loud crunching and metal scraping sound shifted my attention to the steep embankment. I stared in disbelief as a door slid open in the face of the mountain, with a tunnel that appeared just big enough for the Jeep.

"Wait a minute. What's that?" I whispered. My heart beat erratically, and I had to remind myself to breathe.

"This is where we live." Archer's gaze searched my face. "Welcome to Samara."

"Samara?"

"Yes. It means mountain home."

I gripped my chest in an attempt to quiet the loud thudding. My hands began to shake.

"Don't freak out. It's really nice in there. You'll like it."

"No. I think I have claustrophobia." I took a few quick breaths. "I take that back. I know I do." I nodded, hoping to convince them not to drive forward. My stomach sank, and my chest tightened, certain a panic attack was in my near future.

Archer took my hand in his. "It's open and spacious once you get past the tunnel. We have hundreds of thousands of tube holes built into the mountain so it has natural light. It doesn't feel cramped or crowded in any way."

"How big is it? On the inside I mean," I squeaked out.

"We've built three hundred and fifty thousand square feet spread throughout a square mile." Archer smiled. "It's huge."

"Wow." Maybe I could deal with huge.

"Everyone who lives here has about a thousand square feet of living space," he added.

"How did you . . . Never mind. I don't think you'll answer anyway."

"Samara has been here for over five hundred years," Archer continued.

"What?" My mouth dropped open. "How could that be?"

"Question and answer time is over. You gonna go into meltdown if I drive in there?" Devon asked with his usual impatient tone.

*Yes.*

"No," I answered.

# CHAPTER 3

THE JEEP JOSTLED OVER the last few feet of road before the entrance. My sweaty, right hand stayed glued for dear life to the door handle, which ratcheted up the pain in my shoulder tenfold.

*Not smart.* I relaxed my hold.

Devon turned his head back in my direction again, his eyes resting on my shoulder. "You'd better get some pressure on her wound; it's starting to bleed again." He grabbed a package out of his first aid kit and threw it back to Archer. "Make sure to press down firmly."

"Ann, close your eyes. It'll make it easier," Archer said.

"Ann?" The name didn't sound familiar. "My name is Ann? Are you sure?"

"God, Archer." Devon glared at Archer before his dark eyes shifted toward me.

"What? She should know her own name. Or is that secret, too?" Archer smacked his fist against the door. The action startled me at first. But I figured Archer was frustrated because he wanted to protect me. With his beautiful green eyes and genuine smile, yeah, I'd guess any girl on the planet would want him as their personal ally.

"Guys! The name is fine. It just didn't sound right at first for some reason."

Archer's eyes searched mine. "I'm sorry for the slip."

"It's okay."

At least I had one friend.

A buzzing sound overhead had me looking out the window and up toward the sky.

"Just great." Devon groaned.

"What was that?" I asked

"A drone," Archer answered.

Devon shouted, "Duck! They're just over the hill."

I bent forward. "Who are we hiding from?"

"The Jacks."

Ugh. Them again?

"Floor it. Let's get out of here," Archer shouted.

"Hang on." Devon yelled as the Jeep sped forward. We went up a small incline and into the opening. Once inside, there was another loud screech of metal against metal as the doors closed, blanketing us in darkness. I let myself relax for a moment before I realized we were inside and I couldn't see a thing.

"I thought you said there was natural sunlight in here," I said to Archer as beads of moisture formed on my forehead.

He squeezed my hand. "After the tunnel."

Floodlights came to life, illuminating the small area. It was impressive for a tunnel. I just didn't want to have to travel through it. Red bricks covered the semi-circle from top to bottom. The grout between each brick almost sparkled, like they'd just completed an upgrade. It even smelled good, like rain on concrete. I made an internal checklist. Heart rate—good. Breathing—normal. Sweat—under control. Panic attack—not going to happen. Right shoulder—bad.

"Just a few more minutes and we'll see Doc. He'll fix you right up," Archer said.

"Okay." My first feelings of claustrophobia didn't follow me, thank goodness. As we traveled through the tunnel, the structure fascinated me. An architectural work of art—perfectly round with bricks spaced evenly. After another couple hundred feet, the Jeep came to a stop. Again, Archer jumped out and walked up to the next set of metal doors. He put his hand on a pad next to the doorframe. An opening in the panel shot out, and a laser light zoomed right into his eyes.

"You guys weren't kidding about the privacy thing."

Devon rubbed his forehead.

*God, she's killing me.*

"What? Who's killing you?" I asked.

Devon quit rubbing his head, and his body stilled. He turned slowly and stared at me.

Archer returned to the car and took his seat next to me. "All set. Let's go see Doc." He gave my leg a pat and looked up when he noticed Devon wasn't moving. "Devon, I said let's go." When he didn't get an answer, he asked, "What's wrong with him? Were you two fighting?"

"No. I just asked him a question. He said someone was killing him, and I asked who."

"Devon?" Archer asked.

"I have a headache, that's all. I said it was killing me."

I gaped at him. Why did he lie?

"Oh, well, maybe you can have Doc take a look at you, too," Archer offered.

"I'll be fine."

After passing through the set of doors, the Jeep made a swerve to the right, and everything opened up. A huge parking garage with fluorescent lighting that illuminated hundreds of cars spread out before us. Devon pulled into a parking space right next to a set of elevators. He rummaged through his backpack and pulled out another electronic device, pushed a button, and spoke into it. "We have her. We're in."

"Aren't you going to add 'mission accomplished'?" I asked.

Archer turned his face down to look at his hands, his lips pressed together. He gave up and laughed. "Devon, you did sound a little James Bond-ish."

"Try to remember this isn't a joke. She's injured, and we need to get her transported right away." His piercing gaze studied us both. I hadn't noticed it before, but his eyes were dark blue, not black like I'd thought. I tried to look closer, but he shut them for a moment and shook his head.

He was right; my shoulder had begun to throb again even though it had stopped bleeding. Once the bullet injury was taken care of, hopefully someone would tell me what had happened—mainly, why I was in this strange place.

First, I had to ask, "Please, I don't want to go any farther without knowing about the Jacks. Who or what are they?"

They sat stone-faced and didn't answer. I crossed my arms and stared at each one. A few minutes passed. "Well?" I broke the silence.

Archer glanced at Devon. He gave a slight nod.

"The Jacks want to wipe us off the planet. They send out drones on a regular basis, trying to locate our position."

"Why?"

"We've been at war with them for years. It's one reason for our compound and our need for security and privacy."

War with some group named the Jacks. What had I gotten myself into? "Why did you bring me here if these Jack people want to kill you?"

"We believe they want you more than us. Take my word for it—you do not want them to find you."

My stomach dropped. "Why would anyone be after *me*?"

"They want to use you to—" Archer began.

"Enough," Devon interrupted.

"Wait. They want to *use* me? For what? And how do I know that's not what *you're* doing?"

"Again." Devon rubbed between his eyes. "The bullets? That should be a small clue for you."

Not just a jerk. An arrogant jerk.

Devon glanced at my shoulder. "We'll help you with your injury first. If you want to leave after that, I'll drive you wherever you want to go."

*I have nowhere to go.* I copied Devon and rubbed between my eyes. Nope, didn't help.

Fear and confusion clouded my thoughts. I hoped I'd chosen the lesser of two evils.

"We need to go now." Devon interrupted my thoughts.

"I'll get her." Archer jumped out of the Jeep and came around my side. He opened my door and reached in to take my hand.

"Quit trying to get close. You're not going to hear anything," Devon said under his breath.

"You know, just because my arm hurts, doesn't mean I'm deaf." I had no idea what Devon was talking about, but I was tired of asking questions when I knew what the answer would be—"Not yet."

I stood and waited for the feeling of light-headedness to return, but it didn't come. Archer had done a good job stopping the blood loss. All I needed now was to get the bullet out of my arm.

"This Doc guy you keep talking about? He's a real doctor, right?" I held my breath a little, waiting for the answer. This could get ugly.

"Of course." Devon motioned to the elevator. "Come on, they're waiting for us."

I wondered if the elevator would take us down into the bowels of the mountain or up toward the peak. The elevator looked high tech, with polished steel doors and a complicated panel of buttons. When we started to ascend, a rush of relief swept through me.

When the doors opened again, it revealed a huge, open room as large as a football field, but we definitely were still inside the mountain. The bronze, domed ceiling had to be fifty feet high, with tiny streams of sunlight crisscrossing throughout the area. The entire room was like a work of art. Murals of famous paintings covered almost every square inch. Breathtaking, light, and airy. Overstuffed chairs and wooden tables, potted plants, a small cafe, a few TV screens, and what appeared to be a small garden in the back corner gave the room a relaxed feel. But I was far from calm.

*This* was located in the center of a mountain? The amount

of work that went into this must have been staggering. I moved forward a step so I could see a little more. People milled around. Lots of people. I shrank back into the corner of the elevator. All these people were strangers. I wanted to go home.

*You don't have a home anymore.*

"They won't bite." Devon reached for my hand, but I pulled back. I didn't want him to touch me. Strange things happened when he did. And even though it felt good, it scared me.

"Give me a minute." I bent over and placed my hands on my knees.

*Panic attack, please, not now.*

"Let's take the transvater option. We can bypass the Hub for now. Doc can have someone else pick up the water." Archer pressed a few more buttons.

The doors closed again, to my relief. I stood straight, and, this time, the motion was different. Instead of vertical feeling, we moved sideways. I checked both their faces, and they seemed okay with the weird motion. I held onto the side to keep my bearings.

"It's called a magnetic levitation elevator. It's German technology—quite inventive." Archer smiled. "You can let go of the wall; it's perfectly safe." Taking my hand, he said, "Here, hang on to me."

I clasped his hand and balanced against him—just in case.

Devon turned his back to us and pushed a few more buttons. "This will get us a few feet from Doc's office. You won't have to walk far." He didn't turn back around.

*She's too much for me.*

"Who are you talking about?" I asked Devon.

"Uh, Devon didn't say anything." Archer answered for him, his tone uncertain.

I turned toward Devon. "You said someone was too much for you, right?"

Devon stared straight at Archer. "There's no possible way."

Archer shook his head. "Impossible."

"No one has ever . . ."

# CHAPTER 4

"NO ONE HAS EVER what?" I asked.

They stood motionless, eyes and mouths wide open.

"I'm not speaking Greek. Why are you staring at me like that?"

Devon began to pace the small area while he rubbed his jaw.

"Why is she too much?" Archer narrowed his gaze at Devon. "Did you have that thought?"

"Because . . . because she's driving me crazy with all her questions." He stopped pacing and crossed his arms. Soon after, his foot started to tap.

Why was he so nervous?

I turned back to Archer and asked, "What do you mean 'thought'? He said it loud and clear. You heard him, right?"

"Heard what?" an older gentleman asked. The elevator doors had opened.

"Nothing," Devon said through clenched teeth.

Archer coaxed me forward with slight pressure on my back. "Dad, this is Ann. Ann this is my father, Dean Gallagher."

"Pleased to meet you." I stretched out my hand to yet another striking, albeit, older man. Mr. Gallagher stood six feet tall with short, blond, wavy locks like his son. His eyes were steel-gray and determined.

He glanced at my shoulder and said, "Good God, Archer, she's bleeding. What were you thinking? Let's get her into the clinic." His brow furrowed, and his hand replaced Archer's on my back, guiding me out of the elevator.

The large corridor was well-lit, just like the Hub. The floors were polished wood, and the walls appeared to be typical drywall. A door burst open on the right side of the hallway, and a short man with gray hair hurried out.

Mr. Gallagher did the introductions. "Doc, this is Ann."

Doc seemed to ignore Mr. Gallagher and said, "Finally! What took you so long? Where's—oh, there you are young lady. Come with me. I'm all ready for you."

His glasses had slipped down his nose, reminding me of a mad scientist. With quick hand movements, he motioned. "Come on, come on! Let's get you in here."

I stood still. I didn't want to go; there could be more pain. Archer's dad gave me a gentle push forward.

*Brave. I must be brave.*

So many things were happening at once, I needed time to think and get my bearings. Panic wrapped its unwelcome arms around me. My head spun, and someone wheezed in the background.

Me?

And then the world went black.

Voices cut through the darkness.

*She should've been brought in on a stretcher.*

*We had no idea. She seemed to be doing okay.*

*She's tough.*

*Thank God the Jacks didn't get her.*

*We think her parents put a contingency plan in place.*

*How much does she remember?*

*Nothing. She remembers books—that's it.*

*Books?*

*She said she's a reader.*

*She doesn't know she's one of us?*

*No. But, Doc, I don't think she is one of us. She's different.*

*What do you mean?*

*I think she might be . . .*

The scratchy feeling tickling the back of my throat finally burst through, and I coughed. Bad timing. I wanted to eavesdrop some more. Three shadowy figures straightened and stopped talking. The dim lighting didn't allow me to see their faces, but I knew who they were.

The doctor approached the bed and asked, "How are you feeling?"

"I don't know," I answered.

He chuckled. "I guess it's a little early, but let me assure you, you'll be just fine. I removed the bullet from your arm. The entry was clean, not hitting anything major, so you won't have any permanent damage."

"That's good." Permanent damage? I hadn't even

considered it. When my memory left, it appeared all my normal thought processes went with it. I glanced at the IV needle taped to my arm.

"You were dehydrated, and we're administering antibiotics."

"Thanks."

"Archer, Devon, you can leave now. In the morning, she should be feeling well enough for visitors."

"But—"

"No, Archer. She'll be fine. I'll need to spend some time with her before she's introduced to our group."

Archer approached my bed. "Don't worry. You're in good hands with Doc."

"Okay." But my racing heart and sweating palms proved otherwise.

Archer smiled, patting my hand before leaving with Devon. Emptiness followed their departure. They were so different, in both looks and personality, but their back and forth arguing, along with their hovering, distracted me from thinking about all that had happened.

I turned toward the doctor and sighed. "I guess it's just you and me."

With a warm smile, Doc sat next to my bed. "Do you feel like talking?"

"I'm afraid I don't have much to talk about." I pointed to my head. "I have some memory issues."

"I've heard." He paused. "I'm a medical doctor, but I'm also a psychiatrist, mental health counselor, social worker, and a family therapist."

"Wow. Overqualified much?" I smiled.

"I've had lots of time for studies."

"If I talk to you, will you be able to help me get my memories back?" A glimmer of hope began to take form.

"I don't know. But maybe I can help clear up some things and answer some of your questions. There's a lot you need to know."

His eyes held a youthful energy, even though my best guess would place him around fifty. Handsome, with salt and pepper hair, he exuded kindness through his knowing eyes and gentle expression.

*Trust him,* the same voice said.

I wondered if hearing little messages was a common phenomenon with physical and emotional trauma. Could I be soothing myself in some way? I ignored it—again—and continued with my questions.

"I want to know everything."

"Part of my job is to give you the information in palatable bites. I'll give you pieces, let you settle with it, and add more when you're able."

"I can handle it." But I knew, deep down, small bites would probably be best.

He smiled. "I have no doubt."

"First question. Why do I remember some things and not others?"

"Memory loss can take on many forms. Some people can recite every president and not know their spouse of twenty years. It depends on which part of the brain is affected or injured—whether it's caused by an accident or emotional trauma. In your case, we won't know for a few weeks what your knowledge base is. You'll most likely find you have a good amount of understanding in some areas, but in others, a total blank. Don't push yourself. Let things unfold naturally, and you can add as you go."

"Okay," I answered, but I was pretty sure I'd push it. I wanted answers.

# CHAPTER 5

"I'M MORE THAN READY," I said after a two-hour nap and another hour of coaxing.

"Do you remember anything about your parents?" he asked.

"No. Just a flash of their faces. Or, at least, I think it's my parents." I tried to conjure the picture back, but could only envision a fuzzy outline.

Doc paused and looked down at his hands. "I'm terribly sorry to tell you, but your parents died recently."

Not ready.

Where was the oxygen? My heart squeezed, and I couldn't catch my breath. Even though I was lying down, it felt like I'd just run a race. The machine hooked to my arm started to flash, and an alarm went off. A nurse burst into the room and asked, "What happened?"

"I'll need midazolam, right away," Doc told his nurse.

"No. I don't . . . I don't need anything."

His brow wrinkled. "If you can get your breathing back to normal, I'll hold off. You're hyperventilating. Do you know what that means?"

"Yes, not enough carbon dioxide." I focused on taking one breath at a time. How could I remember such an arbitrary detail, but not who I was?

The nurse returned with a long hypodermic needle on a tray.

"It's okay, Maari. I think we can hold off." Doc sat back in his chair and waited.

After a few minutes, when my body started to calm, I said, "I can't remember anything."

"You wouldn't have had such a strong reaction if you didn't have some memory of your parents."

I nodded. "What do you think happened? To my memory—do you know?"

"My best guess is you suffered some sort of major shock. I think whatever happened is too painful for you to grasp, and you're protecting yourself. It's probably a good thing . . . for now, anyway."

"Will you tell me how they died?" I asked.

"Yes. But I'd like to give you a little more time to prepare yourself. Are you okay with that?"

If I had these overwhelming feelings with just the thought of it, I couldn't imagine what I'd be like with details. "Yeah, that's probably not a bad idea." But, still curious, I asked, "Is there anything else you can tell me?"

"Instead of trying to delve into your past, we'll talk about where you are now. I think that's safer territory." He stood and added, "I have something to show you." He left the room and returned with a large, leather-bound book. He placed it next to me on the bed and opened it. "This is one of our first books."

A lungful of air helped calm my nervous stomach, and I sat up to get a better view. The book appeared old and worn, almost ancient. "It's beautiful." Although the printing was light, I could still make out some of the words.

"It is." He flipped a page. "I'll start at the beginning."

"The beginning is always good."

He eyed me.

"I can handle that much, I'm sure."

"It's a lot to grasp," he said.

"Go for it." I smiled to reassure him.

He cleared his throat. "Whatever I tell you today is the truth. There is no reason for me to lie." He paused and continued. "There's a group of us—we're called The Readers."

*That name.* "Yes, I heard about it at the beach." I waited. No flashbacks of books, and my parents' faces didn't appear. Sadness about losing them hung with me though.

Doc noticed my expression and gave my hand a reassuring squeeze. To my surprise, emotion welled within me at his genuine sympathy. I hadn't realized until that moment how much I needed someone to understand.

"I can't grieve my parents properly. I feel their love, but I can't connect it with any memories."

"You will. Give it time."

"Thank you." I took a deep breath and composed myself. "So you like to read, huh?"

"It's not what you think. We read books, lots of them, but that isn't why we have the name."

"I'm a reader. The only memory I have is of this beautiful library filled with books." I caressed the binding. "They looked a little like this one."

"You also read other things." He tilted his head. "I think you might know what I'm saying."

"Other things?" I didn't think I wanted to know. My hands started to shake. So many strange things had happened since I'd woken up on the shore. These people, this place . . . it was too much.

*They will help you.*

The voice. I didn't want to hear it.

*Shut-up.*

"Yes." He laid his hand on the page. "I have a story to tell you, so listen carefully."

I nodded.

"Our group—The Readers. We read minds." He sat perfectly still, waiting for my response.

"Sure. Yeah. That's cool." I kept my face neutral so he wouldn't get a hint of how I felt. *No way.* The idea of escaping this place before they had me drink the Kool-Aid flashed through my mind. The turns we took through the neighborhood came back to me in full, high-definition color. Almost like a map. Hmm. Did I have a photographic memory? *Ironic.*

"It is—cool. But I have a feeling you're not buying it," he said.

"Well, to be honest, I'm not. I think I'd remember that."

"You don't remember ever reading minds?"

My stomach dropped. *You heard Devon's thoughts. You didn't imagine it.*

"Okay. Let's say I heard a thought or two. Maybe from Devon. What does that mean exactly?"

"Devon? That can't be."

"Why not? Unless he teased me. Would he do that?" Devon didn't seem like a practical joker, and why would Archer go along with it?

"No one can read the mind of a Reader. We've perfected the art of blocking for many, many years. Devon and Archer are specially trained for field work, which makes them the strongest in our group. You couldn't hear any of their thoughts, unless . . ." His expression fell off, as though he recalled a better place or time. A slight smile and a flash of hope crossed his face before he shook himself out of it. "Let's get back to discussing blocking."

"What is blocking exactly?" I asked.

"It's a skill that protects us in a couple different ways. First, we can keep our thoughts private. It also helps to keep us focused when we're on the outside. Unwanted thoughts can be quite distracting. You also have this skill," he said.

"I do?"

"Yes, it appears you've been taught by your parents. Devon and Archer tried to read you, and so have I. Even while you were under sedation, your thoughts were silent."

Thank goodness.

"You can read the thoughts of everyone else?" I asked.

"In the general population, yes. But it can be quite distracting, even disturbing."

"How so?" I rubbed my forehead. My headache continued to pester and interfere with normal thought.

"For some, it can be life-threatening. The ones who've made

it this far have been through a lot. But we're human for the most part. We deal with the same emotional issues," he explained with a broad gesture, "as everyone else in the world."

*Dear God. Please tell me I'm not one of these Reader people. Please let Devon's thoughts be a fluke.*

"We still have the same battles as any other person on this planet. We aren't aliens after all." He shrugged and smiled.

Okay. That was a relief.

"No?" I couldn't resist teasing him a little.

He chuckled. "You don't believe me yet. That's all right. This has been a lot to absorb in a short amount of time. Anyway, we haven't moved past the challenges every human has. Anger, jealousy, love, hate, sadness—we struggle with them just like everyone else. We've evolved intellectually over the years, but we haven't been able to control the basic emotions."

"If you controlled them, would they still be considered emotions?"

A huge grin lit his face. "I knew I liked you. No, they wouldn't. That would make us no better than robots. But it has caused some trouble."

I could only imagine.

"Yeah?" I asked.

"Some of us weren't able to handle the emotional burden. I'll save that for another time. I think you've had enough for one day. We'll have an hour session every day from this point on. Write down your questions, and we'll tackle a few during our talks."

Could I handle the emotional burden?

*You were created for this.* The voice . . . again.

"Doc, I'm going to ask you a question that may sound odd."

"That will make us even now, won't it?" He patted my shoulder. With that small contact, I knew I could trust him. Peace filled me, and I wasn't afraid anymore.

"Do you hear voices in your head? Like guiding-type voices?"

"Guiding-type voices?" His brow lifted.

That would probably mean no then.

"Yes, like, 'you go, girl' type messages. Or warning ones."

"It could be stress." He stopped and turned toward me. His expression remained calm. Maybe too calm. "No," he whispered, seeming almost in a trance.

"What? What do you mean—no?"

"Never mind." He shook his head and rubbed his face.

"Can I ask one more question?" I wanted to squeeze out as much as I could.

He glanced at the clock. "One more."

"You keep telling me you've been around for years. Does that mean, like, fifty or a hundred . . . or longer?"

"We're immortal, Ann," he said.

"Immortal? That would mean—"

"We don't die."

# CHAPTER 6

"DO YOU FEEL UP for a walk?" Doc asked.

"Are you trying to distract me? What do you mean you don't die?"

"Come on, I have something to show you."

I pulled the hospital gown around me. "There won't be any social visits will there?"

He laughed. "No, just the two of us."

"Okay." I grabbed his arm and hopped out of the bed, steadying myself. I waited for the dizziness, but it didn't return.

"It's just a few doors down the hall. If you need to sit down or rest, let me know." He studied me, making sure I was good to go.

"Lead the way, Captain." I gave a little salute. Although still a little loopy from the operation, I felt pretty good.

Doc smiled and shook his head. Once we were out in the

corridor, it was only a few steps to our destination. "This is my library. I think you'll like it."

He opened the door, and I walked inside.

"Wow. I mean, wow." Books everywhere. The room was similar to my vision, but also very different. The books were old and musty, and there were thousands of them. "These aren't normal books, are they?"

"You're right. These are more like diaries, a history of our group from the beginning. Well, the beginning of the written word." His gaze over the room was filled with love.

"Can I read them?" I asked.

"Yes. You can come here anytime you like. This room, our history, is open to you." His hand gestured to the shelves.

"Will they tell me why you don't die?" That little bomb he dropped wasn't getting past me.

"Yes, but I can tell you. We only die if we are involved in an accident, murdered . . . situations out of our control." He folded his hands together. "But we don't age like other people. We've conducted scientific research since the nineteen-fifties to see if we could isolate the genetic mutation that occurred during our evolution. We have ten Readers still working on it."

*Don't freak out.*

"A genetic mutation? That's what you are?"

He smiled and put one of the books back on the shelf. "In a nutshell, yes."

"So, let me get this straight. You've been alive since, when, forever or something?" It would be impossible to believe if I hadn't been in the room. Eternal life seemed to emanate from the stories hidden behind the ancient bindings.

"No." He chuckled. "Not forever. We have a beginning. Our

memories reach back to the period right after the last ice age, about ten thousand years ago. We've been evolving since. Our brains have matured within our bodies, unlike our counterparts that evolved through different generations. Back then, we lacked the refinement or sophistication we have now. As a result, our memories aren't as clear."

"Has everyone with this genetic mutation lived the same amount of time? If so, why do you look older?"

He put his hand over his heart. "I do?"

Uh oh.

He laughed when he saw my face drop. "I'm an elder, that's why. I was born in the first wave of mutations. The aging process seems to have stopped for us when our bodies reached the human age of around fifty. The second wave of mutations lasted for a couple hundred years, and, with those Readers, the aging process stopped at about eighteen-years-old. "In the beginning, because we didn't know the power we had, we still interacted with everyone else on the planet. Children were born, families formed. But this created a problem. With the mixing of the races, a few more mutations were formed. We had three different races—all who believed they were superior."

"That doesn't sound good."

Was I actually beginning to believe this?

"It wasn't. There were wars, and an entire race was wiped out."

"What do you mean, a race?"

"The Seers. They could see the future. They were a talented bunch. Quite helpful." He shook his head, and his eyes softened. "There are still a few watered-down descendants. You know them as psychics."

"You mean those people can actually see the future? They aren't just trying to make a buck?"

"Some of them are the crooks and liars you believe them to be. But no, not all. A few have the gift. But it isn't anywhere near the pure version of their forefathers. The Readers survived, but, unfortunately, another group did as well."

"Another mind-reading group?"

"No, the other group is the Hijackers. We call them the Jacks for short."

"Oh. Archer and Devon told me about them. They said the Jacks might be after me?"

"Ahh. That. We're not sure about their motives yet. What we do know is, that given the chance, they'd wipe us off the planet, just like they did to The Seers." He stared off in the distance.

"Why would the Jacks want to wipe you out?"

"They didn't at first, mind you. We all worked together as a unit. The Seers would let us know when there was trouble. Like an earthquake, fire—well, mostly natural disasters because man hadn't created their own disasters yet. We, The Readers, would read the minds of the people affected by an upcoming disaster, and, if they didn't plan on taking immediate action, the Jacks would go in and change their minds. We worked together like this until the big war." He pointed to the corner of the room. "That section over there. There's where you'll find all the information about the battles."

"How big was it?" My heart raced. Could all this be true?

"I'll get to that in a minute. To understand, you'll need to know a little more about the Jacks. Their mutation was different. While we could keep our bodies young indefinitely, they aged and died like everyone else. Unless, of course, they could hijack another human and use the body as their own."

"Wha . . . what?"

"They've survived since the beginning doing this. . . ."

"They sound like that movie. *Invasion of the* . . . oh, what was the name?"

"*Body Snatchers.* There's one big difference."

"What's that?"

"They aren't alien. And, once they settle into their new body by killing the human soul, it's almost impossible to distinguish what they've done. They've created havoc for many, many years." He went to a side table, poured us both a glass of water, and handed one to me. "But I'll let your history class fill you in."

"Class?" I almost choked on my water.

"School. You'll start in a few days once you feel better."

A few days? I needed to get past the next few minutes.

"I just have one more question. Why do they want to wipe out The Readers?"

"When we saw what they were up to, we began to stop them. For whatever reason, we have the gift of eternity, and the Jacks were jealous and fearful. They aren't capable of hijacking a Reader, so now we're seen as a threat to them. As time played out, we've become the protectors of the planet, and they want to destroy us."

I tipped my head to the side.

"We plan to stop them by any means necessary."

"You mean . . . you'd kill them?"

"Yes."

"Am I in the middle of some war between the two races? Is

this some sort of holy war?"

"Yes and no. We believe in good and evil."

"Okaaay . . ." Oops. That sounded snarky.

"You're welcome to think what you want. But make no mistake, this battle is real, and if we don't win—mankind will be lost forever." His grave expression made me regret what I said.

"Sorry, I didn't mean to doubt you. I'm trying to process everything. It's just that, well, this whole story is a lot to take in."

"Every soul on this planet is born with free will, and just like everyone else, we make mistakes."

He motioned to the door. "You've been through a lot today. Let's get you settled into your room so you can mull this over. Do you think you can walk a few more hallways?"

After what he just told me, I was pretty sure I could run. As far and fast as possible to get out of here.

*This is where you belong.* That guiding voice again.

*I'm ignoring you, so you can stop now.*

"Yes, I can make it." Physically, I felt good; emotionally was another subject.

# CHAPTER 7

AFTER THE ELEVATOR ZIGZAGGED through a maze of tunnels and buildings, we finally arrived at our destination.

The corridor, like everywhere else, had high ceilings with natural light coming through hundreds of tubes.

I craned my neck. "How tall are they?"

Doc chuckled. "I have a feeling you'll never get bored here."

"Why is that?"

"It will take a century to answer all your questions."

"Ha ha."

"The ceilings are twenty feet high. It's important for all who live here to have the feeling of light and openness. The human mind is fragile. We've learned this the hard way over the years."

I tilted my head.

He looked away and rubbed the back of his neck. "There have been deaths." His eyes revealed a pain so intense, it shot to my core. I wished I hadn't asked that question. A vision of a lovely girl, maybe twenty years old, dancing in a meadow, flashed before it faded away. What was that? A memory?

"Someone close?" I asked.

"Yes. They all were." He breathed deeply and ran his fingers through his hair. Composing himself, he stopped in front of a door. "Here you are, room 777." He swung it open.

I walked inside, taking in the large room. I loved it. High ceilings and open floor plan, plantation-style furniture, with a carved teak mantel and surround framing a . . . fireplace?

"Is that just for show?" I ran my fingers over the dark wood millwork.

"It's a working fireplace. We keep the temperature regulated, but some people like the extra warmth and coziness of a crackling fire. We have a system to recycle the smoke back into the kitchen and use it for fuel. One of our runners found this technology in an East Indian factory. We travel there quite a bit. They're quite inventive." Pride showed on his face.

"Look at this kitchen." Granite countertops and all the modern appliances made it both functional and beautiful. Was that one of those fancy espresso machines in the counter? "How do you get everything in here?"

He smiled. "Trucks."

"Stupid question." I laughed.

I stopped. The wall on the opposite side of the room had floor-to-ceiling shelves stuffed with books. I approached slowly, running my hands over the spines. A happiness I couldn't define washed over me. I turned and took a closer look the room. Decorated in shades of blue and green, it had just a few feminine touches. With a comfy, oversized chair, woven rugs, and an afghan draped over the corner of the couch—it was perfect.

Too perfect.

A knot began to form in my stomach. "You knew I was coming."

"We hoped you'd come." He shook his head. "But not under these circumstances."

"Have you been . . . watching me, I mean . . . us?" The knot tightened.

"We've kept a watchful eye on you, but only for your protection. We knew *of* you, and that you were possibly one of us." His eyes didn't waver.

"If we were Readers like you, why didn't you protect my parents?" My throat constricted.

"We'd just found out. Your parents ran an article in their university paper about telekinesis and mind-reading. We believed it might be their signal to us for help, but had to be sure. We watched and waited." He continued to rub his hands through his thick, grey hair. "But we were too late. I'm so sorry, Ann."

I nodded, taking everything in. "I'm sure it wasn't your fault. Are you sure I'm one of your Readers?"

"You've lost your memory. The only way to convince you would be to introduce you to the general population on the outside. I'm already convinced, but it would only take about five minutes before you'd know what I told you is true."

"Five minutes? When can we go?" The idea of it was both terrifying and exciting.

"Soon. As I said, for some Readers, it can be overwhelming. The fact we can't hear your thoughts lets us know you're not only a Reader, but a powerful one. Usually, when we find a new Reader, they don't have the skill of blocking yet. Your parents have done a good job." His smile reassured me.

"How does the blocking skill work?" I went over to the espresso machine and fiddled with it.

"It's like breathing to us; no one can get through. Except . . ."

"Except?" I popped in a cup and pressed the button. That was almost too easy.

"We'll talk about that soon." He smiled again.

More information I wasn't ready for. But at least now I could have a cup of hot coffee.

"How do you know I'm not one of those Jack people?" I held my breath, waiting for his answer.

"We sent our best, Archer and Devon, to find and evaluate you. They couldn't hear your thoughts, so that's when they knew you were one of us. The Jacks aren't mind-readers. They don't have the ability to block."

I wasn't a Jack. One bit of good news for the day.

"Do you want a cup of coffee? This machine is great." I held up my cup.

He smiled and shook his head.

I remembered the tingly feeling I had when Devon touched me and wanted to ask him about it, but no—it was too embarrassing.

"I wish I had my memory. It's hard for me to know what's real."

He patted my hand. "Just concentrate on getting better. Right now, it's not important for you to believe what I've told you. I do want you to know we are all here to help and keep you safe."

"Thanks for everything, Doc." I tried to stifle a yawn, but it didn't work. Ten more minutes and the coffee would kick in.

"Try to rest. I'll have Devon and Archer pick you up first thing in the morning. You'll need a tour around Samara."

"Why both?" I didn't want Devon around me. He made me feel all sorts of uncomfortable with the dark, brooding way he had about him.

"Why not?" Doc eyed me.

"I don't know." How to put this? "I don't think Devon likes me very much. He's grouchy around me."

Doc's head tipped back, and he let out a chuckle. "He's like that with everyone. He has the weight of the world on his shoulders. At least, that's what he thinks."

"What does that mean?"

"Among other things, it's his job to find the lost Readers. He's found three in the last hundred years."

"And because I'm a Reader, I've been brought here for my protection." I put my cup back on the counter.

He nodded. "Exactly."

"What if it's proved I'm not one of your Readers, what then? Will you kill me?" I braced for his answer.

"Of course not!" He stood straighter. "Our goals are to save lives, not take them."

"I could be a fluke of nature. What if you're wrong about me? I'm a witness. I know where your compound is. You'd just let me go?"

"We'd have two choices. One, we'd move our compound to another location. The second, you'd agree to stay." His eyes remained focused on mine, unwavering.

"You'd move your entire compound just so I could go back to living a normal life?" My eyes swept around the room, taking in the expert craftsmanship, the opulence, and painstaking details.

"Yes, we would. We have time. We'd move back after—" He stopped abruptly.

Realization struck. "Oh, I get it. If I'm not a Reader, I'll die like everyone else."

He smiled and gave my shoulder a pat. "Don't worry about it right now. We'll take baby steps, one at a time." I stared into his eyes, hoping the truth shining back at me was real.

"I think I can handle that." But could I?

"Goodnight, Ann. And welcome."

"Thanks, Doc." I shut the door along with all the insanity.

Was it insane though?

The sedative used for the operation hadn't completely worn off, but the adrenaline ricocheting through my veins made me anxious. I paced the room. Could any of what he said be true? Or was I in a high-tech version of what some mad scientist had created? Even without my memory, I had a sense of what the real world was like, and it didn't involve mind-reading, hijackers, and seers.

I strolled around the room, appreciating the care that went into decorating it. I had to give it to them, they certainly had me pegged. I could imagine myself staying here for a long time. But forever? If it were true, and I was a Reader, would it mean I wouldn't die of old age? Would that be a good thing?

With my mind racing, but my body tired, I needed to switch off my internal monologue. I couldn't figure everything out in one day. It was best to block out all I'd heard and try to sleep. I walked back to the kitchen and poured out the rest of my coffee.

Where was the bedroom? I looped around the room twice before spotting a small red button next to a door with no handle. I pressed it and moved back just in case. It opened up into another gorgeous room. A plantation-style teak bed sat in the middle on a raised platform, with satin sheets, soft and warm-looking blankets, and comforters piled high. A pair of PJs with a cat pattern sat folded by the pillow. Did I like cats? So far, everything they'd chosen for me was spot-on. Although, I wasn't too excited to become a cat lady. How did I even know about cat ladies? These random bits of memory unsettled me. The PJs were quite cute though. I picked them up and breathed the lavender scent.

Not wasting any time, I put them on and collapsed onto the mattress, allowing exhaustion and comfort to lull me into a restless sleep. The last thought I had before drifting off was that these people sure knew what they were doing.

# CHAPTER 8

POUNDING DRUMS. NO, A pounding hammer . . . on the door?

I rubbed my eyes and tried to clear the fog from my brain. *Where am I?*

"Hey, Sleeping Beauty. Time to get up." Devon's deep voice startled me fully awake.

I sat up, clutching the blanket to my chest. "What are you doing here? Get out!"

"We're your guides for the day." Devon stood over my bed with his arms crossed. Archer leaned against the doorframe and mouthed, 'Sorry.' They both wore faded jeans, but Archer's t-shirt was white and Devon's black.

They must coordinate to match their souls.

I glared at Devon. "You're evil, you know that?"

He turned and started for the door. "Yeah, yeah, I know. You have five minutes. We'll wait for you out here."

Was he joking? Well, if he wasn't, he was in for a rude

awakening. Shower and change in five minutes? Not possible.

He called out in my direction. "Oh, and if you take too long, we'll come in and get you."

"You better be kidding," I shouted back. He chuckled, and a muffled 'no' came through the bedroom door

I jumped out of bed. No way would I go anywhere without a shower. I smelled like salty seaweed combined with antiseptic. Not pleasant. Almost slipping on the tile floor, I stepped into the shower. I gave the one button a forceful jab. The temperature was just right as the water poured down from a rain-shower nozzle. I moved under and let the soft drops soothe away the last twenty-four hours, unwinding and losing track of time, until—

"Are you going to stay in there all day?" Devon asked.

He wasn't? He didn't?

"If you don't get out of here right now, I'll . . . I'll—"

"Hit me with your towel?"

"This is not funny!" I searched around the shower stall for a weapon of some sort. A bar of soap. Hmmm. I could rub it in his eyes.

"I'm not in your bathroom. I'm using the intercom. So you can chill."

I peeked out of the opaque glass door. No one was in the room.

"Very funny. I'll need five more minutes."

"We don't have all day. We're hungry," Devon's impatient voice boomed.

For the first time since yesterday, food sounded good. "You didn't mention food. I'll be right out."

The bathroom connected to a large closet, so I didn't have

to walk past them wearing only a towel. I stopped in the middle of the room. The closet was filled with hundreds of outfits, from dresses to casualwear to workout clothes. Did they raid a department store? There has to be an intercom around here somewhere.

"Um. Guys?" I asked.

"Yeah?" Archer's voice answered.

So, they could hear me. Weird.

"You can't see me, right?"

"No, the intercom is only audio."

"Okay. Who owns these clothes?"

"They're yours. Pick something and let's go." Devon's bossy voice again.

The conversation with Doc came back to me all at once. They'd spent a good amount of time preparing for me. I couldn't think about that now while rushing, so I grabbed the first thing available. Jeans and a pink t-shirt. Simple.

I joined them in the living area. "What's the hurry anyway?"

Archer smiled. "Food. They close in fifteen minutes. This one," his head tilted toward Devon, "can't function without a stack of pancakes."

"True." And then Devon smiled. He had remarkable, good looks when he wore a bored expression. Or a scowl. Or when he was angry, tired, or frustrated. But when he smiled, his face lit up, and he transformed into a ridiculously, absurdly beautiful man. His dark blue eyes, the dimple in his right cheek, perfectly shaped lips, and messy black hair made my brain freeze for a moment.

I stared, and I think my mouth hung open a little.

A blank look replaced his smile. "What?"

I turned away to hide the blush creeping up my face. "Nothing. Lead the way."

We went through the usual twisty elevator ride, and I relaxed a little.

"See? That wasn't so bad, was it?" Archer asked.

"I'm starting to get used to it."

"Good. You'll be a pro in no time." He took me by the arm and escorted me into the Hub.

When we crossed through the doors all activity stopped. Around two hundred people turned to stare—at me.

The little bit of confidence from using the elevator without incident fled, replaced by embarrassment and a good dose of anxiety. The center of attention was not my thing. The silence was deafening.

"Why is everyone looking at me?"

"Hey, everyone. This is Ann. Say hi," Archer shouted to the open room. After a little bit of nervous laughing, clearing of throats, and shuffling of papers, a few "Hi's" chorused from some of the group.

A girl in a stunning green dress that hugged her perfectly-shaped body broke through the crowd, with arms outstretched, and came toward me. "Ann!" She wrapped me into a big hug, squeezing me like a long-lost friend.

"Um . . . hi. Who are you?" I tried to squirm free.

"I'm Lucy. We'll be the best of friends. Right, boys?"

Archer chuckled. "Not if you squeeze the life out of her."

"Oh! So sorry. I've waited so long; it's like I know you already!" She bounced on the balls of her feet. "I'm your liaison. Archer and Devon will give you the tour, and I'll fill you in on everything else."

Her enthusiasm was contagious. She had fire-engine-red hair, a smattering of freckles sprinkled over her high cheekbones and nose, and a smile that should be on magazine covers. I needed to talk to the doctor more about this mutation. It must affect their beauty gene or something.

"Sure, I'm game." I scanned the room, and, sure enough, spread around the large room were people who looked like they were getting ready for a runway in Paris, a beauty pageant, or *America's Next Top Model*. I smoothed my hair, but there was no denying I was out of my element.

After we served ourselves at the buffet, we found an unoccupied table and sat down. Everyone had gone back to their previous activities.

"Archer?" I said quietly, not wanting anyone else to hear.

"Yeah?" he whispered back.

"What's with all the people here? Everyone is so . . . attractive."

He choked a little on his corn flakes.

"Is it part of the mutation the doctor talked to me about?" I asked.

"He told you about that?" Devon asked, a frown shadowing his face.

Great. He has super hearing as well.

"Yes. A little. But I think he held back a lot."

"I would hope so." He scowled.

There was no way I could compare to these people. "It's apparent I don't belong here. If you let me go, I'd never talk about you or reveal the location of Samara. I promise."

"How do you know you aren't one of us?" Archer asked.

"Well, first of all, we don't know if I can read minds yet.

Maybe I'm highly perceptive and caught a thought or two. That isn't conclusive. Also, I don't have the drop-dead gorgeous gene you all seem to share." I surveyed the room again. Thank goodness everyone had gone back to what they were doing.

"You're right about one thing," Archer said. "Your genetic mutation is different. It's more powerful."

That wasn't the answer I'd expected.

"Really? How do you figure?"

"For one, you're much better looking than any of the women around here, or men for that matter."

I laughed and snorted at the same time. How unladylike could I be? I pressed my lips together, but it was too late to take it back.

His voice softened. "When's the last time you looked in a mirror?"

Mirror.

"I'm not really sure. I didn't see one in the bathroom."

"They just completed a remodel and haven't installed it yet," Archer said.

"You mean, you don't know what you look like?" Devon stared like I was crazy.

"Of course." I moved back from the table and grabbed a lock of my hair. "Brown hair, around five feet three inches, and one hundred and ten pounds." At least that's what Doc told me.

"What does your face look like?" He wouldn't stop.

"Normal. Ordinary."

"When was the last time you saw your reflection?" Devon asked.

Reflection? I couldn't draw up a clear picture. The glass door at Doc's clinic was my only impression. Although distorted, it still gave me a good idea of my appearance. And there was no way I compared to these people around me.

"Let's drop it. There's probably a reason for it," Archer said to Devon.

Devon shrugged and lifted his hands. "Whatever."

Lucy joined the conversation. "So, boys, where will you take her first? The kitchens, or will you start with the laundry?" She scrunched her nose. "I hate it when I pull laundry duty."

Lucy bubbled with an excess of energy. How would I ever keep up with her?

"We'll start with the gym and work our way to the boring stuff," Archer said.

"Can I come with you?" She placed her hands together as if in prayer and said, "Please, please, ple-e-e-ease!"

"No," Devon cut her off.

Her lip popped out into a pout. "You're so mean."

"You can't go. You have class in ten minutes."

"Don't remind me." Lucy turned toward me. "The Industrial Revolution. I mean, can machines be any more boring?"

"Lucy, you know it wasn't about the machines. It was the fact they started to replace people." Devon shot her one of his scary laser stares.

She didn't seem to be affected. "Ugh. I know. Can't we just skip to that part?" She picked up a book bag. "Professor Anderson just drones on and on about those contraptions. He said we need to learn about the mechanics in order to decipher at which point the Jacks intervened—" She stopped, bit her lip, and stared at me.

"She does know about the Jacks, right? Tell me someone

has told her." Her eyes widened as her head shifted back and forth between Devon and Archer.

They stared back at her with blank expressions.

"No worries, Lucy. I've been updated. Well, I know a little bit, so you didn't ruin anything."

Her shoulders relaxed. "You two! I about had a heart attack. There *will* be retribution." With that, she slung her bag over her shoulder and stomped out of the Hub.

"Do you do that often?" I asked.

"What?" Devon drew out the word.

"Tease that poor girl. You really scared her."

He shrugged. "That's what sisters are for."

No way.

"You're telling me that girl is your sister. As in blood-relative-type relation?" I couldn't imagine two people who were more polar opposite.

"Yep." He smiled again.

I needed protection from that smile. My heart beat too fast, and heat rose to my face. Evasive action was required.

Thank God they couldn't read my thoughts.

I averted my eyes to the floor just in time to see a little, gray shadow next to my feet. The shadow moved, but I moved quicker. Within seconds, my feet were planted on the chair seat, and there was loud shrieking echoing throughout the room.

I glanced around to see who was making all the noise, but it had stopped.

It was me. I was the one shrieking. Wonderful.

The shadow, which turned out to be a big, hairy rat, darted

out from under our table and across the room.

"That's—that's a rat!" I choked out.

Devon bit his lip, and Archer covered his mouth. I dared my eyes to look around the room, and, once again, everyone stared at me. This time smiles and suppressed grins lined their faces.

Great first impression.

"I don't think he's coming back after all your screaming. You've probably traumatized the little guy." Devon smirked.

"Little guy? What, do you name them here? They're disgusting rodents! Did you see the tail on that thing?" I pointed in the direction it scurried.

"You can come down now. It's safe." Archer had the decency to hide his smile. "We get them from time to time. They are humanely escorted out when they get through. Usually, it's during a delivery or something. By the way, it was a mouse, not a rat."

Information I didn't care about. How they got in didn't matter. It was the fact they were in.

"Come on, off the chair." Devon rolled his eyes and held out his hand.

I crossed my arms and shook my head. "No."

*A small space, almost the size of a coffin. Dark. Narrow. What is that? Oh, God, A rat! I squirm in silent protest as it bites my arms and legs. Get me out!*

I squeezed my eyes shut and tried to block the memory. But I couldn't. The trembling started and turned to shaking within seconds. Two arms grabbed me and carried me from the room.

"Quick, let's get her to Doc's," Archer ordered. "She's having a flashback."

# CHAPTER 9

Doc leaned back in his chair and said, "I think your parents needed to hide you from time to time."

"In a coffin? With rats?" What type of parents would do that?

It's our belief your parents have been protecting you for thousands of years. I'm sure it was probably a small space, not a coffin." His smile remained gentle. "But it would explain your problem with claustrophobia, and your fear of rodents. In this case, a mouse."

I groaned. "He *was* small, wasn't he?"

He nodded.

"Does everyone think I'm crazy?"

"Do you think *we* are?"

"Touché." I laughed for the first time since arriving. "Doc?"

"Yes, Ann?"

"I'm okay now. Can I go back to the tour?"

He pushed his glasses farther up his nose. "Yes. But try to remember, you've been through a lot in a short amount of time. Get a little exercise, but take things slow."

"I think it'll help me to get my bearings." I picked at the hem on my t-shirt. "I feel a little lost here."

"Of course you do." His ageless eyes communicated a kind concern. "It's important for you to look around in order to feel comfortable."

"I'm trying to process everything. That I'm here, in this place." My gaze took in the normal office, with the large wooden desk, comfortable chairs, and diplomas hanging on the walls. "And I don't have a home anymore." I cleared my throat. "And my memory is gone." I wiped the moisture from the corners of my eyes. Would I always be in this limbo?

"Your memory will return when you're ready to deal with it." He handed me a tissue. "I suggest you give yourself a few days to get adjusted, meet some new people . . . and get into a routine. I'm sure, once you settle in, things will start to click into place."

His soothing words helped me get some perspective. I liked it here. Even though they were strangers, there was also a familiarity, a bond of some sort. I liked everyone I'd met so far—well, except for Devon. The jury was still out on him.

A knock at the door.

"Come in."

Archer's smiling face peered around the doorframe. "Is it safe?" he asked.

I laughed and asked, "Why wouldn't it be?" When he came farther into the room, I saw his black eye. "Tell me you didn't get that from me."

"Okay. I won't," he said with a wink.

I gasped, recalling how I struggled when he lifted me off the chair. "I did that?"

He grinned, and even though I had marred his good looks, he was still gorgeous. Blond hair streaked with even lighter shades and combined with the brightest bottle-green eyes I'd ever seen. He stood inside the door frame, all six-foot-three of him, waiting . . . for me.

I gulped.

He walked over to my chair and took my now-sweaty hand. "Don't worry about it. I should've been prepared. I suspected you were having a flashback of some sort."

I pulled my hand free and, covering my face, asked, "Did I punch you?"

Another wide grin, and those beautiful eyes of his did that crinkling thing I loved.

"Nothing as aggressive as that. Just an elbow. You weren't trying to hurt me. You wanted to get away from—"

"I know, I know! Please don't remind me." My skin crawled all over again.

Archer turned to Doc. "Is it all right if I take her on a walk? I'd like to show her around a little."

"Yes, that's a good idea. We're done here."

"Thank you, Doc." I gave him a quick hug. "And thanks for talking to me."

He waved and said, "Have fun."

Archer took hold of my hand again as we left. I tried to tug it free once we were out the door, but he held tight.

Well, okay then.

"I'm taking you to the waterfalls. You'll love them," he said with a reassuring smile.

*Interesting.* "Are the waterfalls inside the compound?"

"You'll see." A sweet expression followed as he led me past the elevator, like a little boy hiding a secret.

"No transvater?"

"No. Walking will strengthen you."

"You're a doctor now?" I lifted an eyebrow.

"Well, actually, yes, I am."

"No. You're teasing me. Really?" I stopped walking.

"I don't practice medicine much anymore. We leave most of that to Doc. I have to pass boards every three years, but most of my studies were done years ago."

"How many doctors live here?"

"Right now, two-hundred-seventy-six of us are licensed doctors, with three more in Med-School. We need the ability to take care of each other." He gave my shoulder a gentle squeeze. "I told you I'd look out for you, and I meant it."

The sincerity in his unwavering gaze made my stomach flip. He moved a step closer, and his eyes dropped to my lips.

I forgot to breathe for a moment.

Lucy rounded the corner. "There you are!"

I took a step back and struggled to regain my composure. "Hey, Lucy. We're about to go to the waterfalls."

She turned to Archer. "The waterfalls." She dropped her chin and raised a brow. "You're taking Ann to the waterfalls?"

"Yes." He stared back at Lucy. Or was that a glare?

"Does Devon know?" Her eyes narrowed, and I swore her hair turned a brighter red.

"Devon's off doing what Devon does." He waved a hand in

the air. "The waterfalls are calming. After what she's been through, I'd think you'd agree."

"Then you won't mind if I tag along, right?" She raised both eyebrows. "I *am* her liaison, after all."

"Skipping classes?" he asked.

"Nope." She flipped her hair back.

They faced each other in a silent showdown.

Archer let out a long breath and said, "Fine. Let's go."

The fire-haired beauty won.

Ten more minutes of walking through open corridors that branched out in every direction had me thinking we'd never arrive. "Are we there yet?" I asked, but it came out high-pitched, like a child. A flush of embarrassment spread across my cheeks.

Archer gave my hand a little squeeze. "You're funny."

"She might not be joking." Lucy stopped and examined me. "You feeling all right?"

"Yes. Yes, I'm sorry for complaining. I feel fine." I glanced back in the direction we'd just come. "Samara is so much bigger than I imagined, like it goes on forever."

"Forever has just ended." Archer opened a large door with a rubber flange that ran around the entire frame, and we stepped inside.

"Holy . . . Wow. How in the world were you able to do this?" We'd entered a different world. A huge room, I'd guess to be around ten thousand square feet, stretched out before me. Green tropical foliage and the perfumed scent of cascading water invited me in. I inhaled the rich aroma and took a closer look around.

I pointed to the waterfall. "That's breathtaking."

"Isn't it? Thirty-feet of power crashing into the lake."

I took off my shoes and stepped into the sand. The soft granules were warm and welcoming.

My head tilted up. "It looks like the sky." Painted blue, the vaulted ceilings soared above us.

"We installed extra light tubes in here. It helps, don't you think?"

"Yeah, I feel like I'm outside. This is incredible." The natural sunlight made me squint. I put my hand over my eyes and continued to look around. At near seventy-five degrees, the temperature made me warm, without being too hot. Moisture gathered on my skin, and the thunderous sound of the rushing water helped me relax.

"Let's grab some chairs and sit next to the lagoon. We're lucky; there aren't many people here today." Lucy started to drag some chairs next to the water's edge. "Next time, Ann, we'll bring swimsuits and go in."

I winced, remembering the last time I was in the water. Not so fun.

"Whenever you're ready," Lucy said, taking my hand and tugging me toward the chairs. Archer still had possession of my other hand.

"Um . . . guys?"

They stopped glaring at each other for a moment and turned toward me.

"My arm kinda hurts."

The release of both my hands was instantaneous. In unison, they both said, "Sorry!"

A beeping sound came from Lucy's hip. She unhooked a small rectangular case and groaned when she read the message. "I have to go." She turned to Archer, pointing at him. "You behave."

He widened his beautiful eyes and set his hand over his heart. "Me?"

She spun back toward me. "Don't worry. I'll be back in ten, fifteen minutes tops." With one more warning glare at Archer, she left.

Archer laughed and rubbed his hands together. "We have fifteen minutes to do all sorts of bad things. What would you like to start with first?"

I raised an eyebrow, and he laughed harder.

"Come on. Let's get a seat and relax before Her Highness returns."

We arranged our beach chairs side-by-side, and I tipped mine back. "This is the perfect place for me today." A familiar, peaceful feeling washed over me, and I closed my eyes.

"Better?" he asked.

"A hundred percent. I've all but forgotten about the hairy monster in the cafeteria. Well, I take that back, I can still see his beady eyes. But I feel much better."

"Good."

My eyes scanned the area again. "This had to have been a lot of work."

"Yeah. The Elders have gone to a lot of trouble to make our lives as normal as possible. They've done a good job."

"What else have they done?" I turned in my chair to face him.

"They've set up a system to make sure everyone has a goal or a job that stimulates them. We avoid boredom at all costs. We keep the cycle different."

"In what way?"

"Our cycles are both work and pleasure related. Readers are sent out in groups to gather information that helps with the running of the compound. We also leave on vacation or sabbaticals. They've made every effort to make life in our mountain as light and real as possible. We need to be out in the world, even if it's in small doses. Usually after two months, we're called back."

"Why two months?"

"That seems to be the best amount of time. It can be emotionally draining to be around thoughts that aren't our own."

"Yeah. Doc told me about that. How do you deal with it? Are you okay?"

A slow grin spread across his face. "Thanks for asking. I'm good."

I returned his smile.

He leaned over and whispered in my ear, "I want to ask you a favor." The scruff on his jaw bristled against my cheek.

I pulled back a little. "What type of favor?"

"Don't make any decisions for at least a month. I think, by that time, you'll have learned who we are and how you fit in."

I studied him for a moment, trying to interpret his words. "What type of decision?"

He looked down and pulled a piece of thread loose from the edge of his t-shirt. His eyes drifted up and met mine. "I'm just going to say it. Please don't put me in the 'friend' or 'like-a-brother' category—not yet, not until we get to know each other. I'm just asking for a chance." He bit his lip and waited.

My heart sped up a little. "But you don't know me. Not

really."

He picked up my hand again. "Don't freak out."

"That sentence alone freaks me out."

More surprises. Just great.

"I was the one they sent to guard your house." He slumped a little. "My two months were up. I was called back just before your parents died. I should've stayed." Rubbing his face, he gazed off into the distance.

"Well, you can't predict the future like a Seer, right? Please don't feel badly."

With a subdued smile, he said, "No. We couldn't have seen it. But I keep thinking I missed something." He shook his head.

"How did you get to know me?" I asked, not sure if I wanted to hear his answer.

"We had cameras with audio."

My mouth dropped open, unnerved knowing strangers had watched us.

Archer placed his hand on my arm. "Don't worry; they were only in the main living areas, and only there for your protection. I never saw you in person though. You never left."

"You mean, in the two months you watched us, I never left the house?" That seemed odd. "Did we know we were in danger?"

He hesitated. "We've all agreed the information you receive about your life would come from Doc. I can't say a lot. But what I can say is, I was able to know you—but not in a creepy, stalker way." He squeezed my hand. "You're strong, Ann. Like no one I've ever met."

I placed my free hand over my face and tried to think.

Something about what he'd said made sense. A familiar emotion edged at the outskirts of my memory. Hiding. That was familiar. I always hid. But why?

*You're special. We have to protect you.*

A memory. Not the annoying voice this time. I didn't know which was worse.

"What was I like? Was I happy?" Tears welled. I blinked them back.

He got up and sat next to me on my lounge chair. With hands cupping my face, he said, "Yes, you were. That's what I admired most about you." He glanced down at my lips again. His lips looked soft and full. I had an urge to feel them against mine.

Definitely not in the friend category.

"I was there, too. You forgot to mention that." Devon's voice cut through the fog. Archer's story had captivated me so much, I hadn't realized anyone else was around.

Archer stiffened, rose, and returned to his chair.

"Really, Archer? The waterfalls? She's been here all of two days." His scowl was deep, his voice impatient.

Archer crossed his arms and glowered at him.

"What's wrong with the waterfa—oh." I hadn't noticed before, but everyone here seemed to be enjoying themselves. *Very* much. Couples were scattered around the beach, in the water, and lying on the sand. All of them . . . cozy. Well, well, well. Archer had taken me on a date? No wonder Lucy had acted so strange. A giggle started low in my belly and made its way up before I slapped a hand over my mouth.

"I didn't bring her here for *that*," he grumbled. "It's been a stressful few days. I wanted her to unwind." He turned to me and asked, "You were relaxing until he showed up, right?"

"A little too much." Devon's glare flipped back and forth between Archer and me.

Heat warmed my cheeks. It was official. *Devon is a jerk.*

"Yes, it's very calming. Thank you for bringing me here, Archer. I appreciate it." I flashed Devon my best 'mind your own business' look and closed my eyes, ignoring them both.

After an hour of drifting in and out of sleep, I heard, "You can leave now, Devon. I'm sure you have better things to do."

"No, I need more relaxing time myself. Good idea, Archer."

"It's not going to work," Archer growled.

"What won't work?" Devon's voice rose a little. Ah, he was playing innocent.

"Babysitting. Things will happen as they should. You know that."

My eyes popped open. "What *things?*"

They both turned toward me as if they just remembered I was there.

Devon ignored me and said to Archer, "I'm hungry. I think it's time for dinner. Sound good?"

"Wait a minute. You're not leaving me?"

They both got up from their chairs, brushed themselves off, and started toward the exit.

"I don't know how to get back!" I called out.

Devon waved me on. "Come on then."

I scrambled and caught up to them. "You were going to ditch me just because I asked a question?" I gave Archer a pointed stare.

He grimaced. "We have a gag order for now. Things are difficult." He held the door open for me. "And no, we weren't going to leave you. Maybe distract you a bit so you'd forget your question."

"Well, I feel *so* much better." I walked ahead of them, but stopped when I realized I had no clue where to go.

"Don't worry, you'll get the hang of it soon." Archer gave my back an encouraging pat.

My frustration put aside for now, I followed them to the Hub. Once we entered, my stomach growled. The food smelled delicious, and breakfast seemed like days ago.

"Here, please sit." Archer pulled out a chair and gave a little bow. "I'll get you a plate. What would you like to eat?"

I flopped down, willing to be pampered a little. "You choose. I'm not picky."

They left on their quest for food. The large space was filled with close to two hundred people, all involved in various activities. Some were having a bite to eat, like us. Others sat at tables and appeared to be studying and working on computers. In one corner, two men played a game of ping pong.

"Hey, I'm Susie." A girl's voice startled me.

"Oh, hi. I didn't see you come up."

"That's okay." She sat in the chair next to me.

I expected a beauty, like all the others, but she was even prettier, if that was possible. Wavy, blond hair that almost sparkled with its shiny gloss. Bright eyes, a pert nose, and white teeth. What was I doing in this place of genetically supreme people?

"I wanted to have a little friendly girl talk with you," she said.

"Okay." Something was off. Maybe her smile?

"Your little performance today? You know the 'Oh, help me, I saw a mouse' one? It's not going to work."

Wow. Jealous much? Doc was right. They hadn't evolved through the basic emotions.

"It wasn't a performance." I pressed my lips together and tried to calm my anger. I glared at her while my nails bit into my palms.

"Give me a break. I'm sure you already know they're like royalty around here, and I won't let some two-bit Reader from who-knows-where undo years of strategy and planning. They're mine."

She said all this through clenched teeth while smiling. I almost applauded.

"Seriously? Both?" I hoped she was joking.

"I haven't decided yet—so, yes. Stay away." She got up from her chair with her stupid, fake smile still plastered on her face. "Or you'll be sorry."

# CHAPTER 10

"OH, ARCHER. DEVON. I'M so happy to see you." The blond Barbie threw her arms around Archer first, avoiding his plate of food, then moved on to molest Devon.

Did they like this she-devil?

"Susie, when did you get back?" Archer asked with a huge smile.

Yes. They liked her. She must be a master at blocking.

"Just yesterday. I tried to find both of you, but you were busy." She shot a glance at me.

"We're never too busy for you," Devon said, winking at her.

Was he flirting with her? If I had food in my stomach, I'd have hurled. Archer put a plate of food in front of me. Funny, I wasn't hungry anymore.

"Have you met Ann?" He looked back and forth between us. Susie had her smile in place, but I wasn't as good an actress. I tried to smile, but the scowl competed for dominance on my face.

She flashed an angelic expression at Archer. "Yes. We just had a lovely talk."

He grinned back. Oh, please. He fell for it.

"That's great. I'm sure you two have a lot in common," he said.

Well, Archer was right about that.

Lucy plopped down next to me at the perfect time, because I was about to blurt out something inappropriate to Miss Perfect Susie Q. I didn't need any enemies my first week.

"I'm so sorry, Ann. I'd hoped to get back to the waterfalls to check in, but we had an emergency." Lucy grabbed a salt shaker and sprinkled her French fries.

"She was at the waterfalls? With whom?" Susie's friendly expression would have fooled most people, but the small tic next to her right eye gave her away.

Devon and Archer shot each other a glance.

Lucy broke the awkward silence. "Archer and Devon are in charge of her initiation. I'm her liaison. Did you have any questions?" She had a great way of maintaining a polite demeanor, without being rude. Lessons were needed; I was ready to suggest organ donation. Her heart specifically. It wasn't doing much for her.

Susie's façade cracked a little. She blinked a few times and said, "That sounds wonderful. I'd love to come on some excursions with you. It's quite exciting to have a new person join us."

"That'd be great." Devon set his tray down on the table and sat across from me. "Would you like to join us for dinner, Susie?"

"No!"

All four pairs of eyes turned to me. I froze, and my heart might have stopped. "I said that out loud, didn't I?"

Lucy stifled a giggle, and her eyes crinkled in merriment. Devon and Archer had matching blank expressions. And Susie, well, her smile was like one of those cats who'd just slurped down a big bowl of milk.

"What I meant to say is, no, I won't be staying for dinner. I've lost my appetite and plan to go back to my room. But I hope all of you enjoy your meal." I got up from the table. Why hadn't they given me a map of Samara? That would have been smart. No matter, I'd walk the halls for hours to get away from Susie.

"I'll go with you." Devon rose from his seat, ignoring his food.

"No, I'll go." Archer got up.

This wasn't good. I put my hand up. "Really, I can go by myself. It's time I learned how to get around without help."

"You two, sit back down." Lucy took hold of my arm. "I'll be her escort. I already grabbed a bite earlier. You can finish your dinner and check on her later." She shoved her plate of French fries toward Devon.

The two looked each other over. Devon was the first to crack with a raised shoulder. Archer nodded, and they both sat.

As soon as we were safely down the hall, Lucy broke down in a fit of giggles. "Oh my gosh. Did that just happen?" She bent over, holding her sides, laughter taking over.

"What's so funny? That was a disaster."

Her giggles turned to snorts and were contagious. "I've waited for years—and I'm talking hundreds of years—for this to happen." She clamped her mouth shut.

"Not you, too. Now you have to tell me." I placed my hands on my hips. That didn't get her talking, so I raised an eyebrow.

"Okay, Okay." Her eyes darted up and down the corridor. "Let's go to your room, where no one will hear us. I'll give you a little background. You're going to find out anyway."

Finally.

I grabbed her arm and started down the corridor. "Don't tell me the turns. I want to see if I can do this on my own." I started and stopped a few times. "I think it would be easier if these hallways didn't all look the same. It's so bland with the walls painted beige and no pictures or anything."

"It's constructed this way on purpose. If we ever had an invasion, the builders hoped these twisty halls without markers would slow the Jacks down." Lucy smiled, and her eyes darted to the turn on my right.

"Thanks for the hint. Are you expecting an invasion?"

"If the Jacks ever found out where we live, then yes. They wouldn't hesitate. They have drones everywhere, but we've remained undetected. I don't think they really know what to look for anyway. They aren't very bright." She winked and smiled, obviously trying to reassure me. It wasn't working.

I fidgeted with my necklace, imagining the halls full of Jacks. Would they be the opposite of The Readers? Ugly monsters with fangs? I shivered.

"We have drills every month and an escape plan in place. They'd likely be roaming around Samara for days before even noticing we were gone."

"What do they look like?" I bit my lip and waited.

She shrugged. "Normal, just like us."

That was somewhat comforting.

"We're here. Good job." She gave me a little pat on my back.

Hmm. A door without a handle. "Thanks. Now I just have to figure out how to get into my room."

"It's easy. See this panel here? You just put your hand on it, and it'll open right up."

I placed my hand on the square wall panel, and, sure enough, the door popped open. "How many people have access to my room?"

"Well, there's me, of course. Archer, Devon, Doc, and the Elders."

Mystery solved. That's how Devon and Archer got into my room this morning. "That's a lot of people. Why so many?"

"It's protocol for all new arrivals. Especially for you, since you've been injured."

"That lasts for how long?"

"Oh, probably not much longer. You're doing so well."

We walked into the room, and the same sense of peace from yesterday settled in again. Odd, it felt like months.

Lucy flounced down on the sofa and patted a spot next to her. With her bright face and squirming body, I knew whatever secrets she planned to spill were good. "Where to start. Where to start." Her index finger tapped against her lips.

"Anywhere! Just get going before I burst." I nudged her and she laughed.

"All right. To make sense of Susie we have to start with the Seers."

"So, you're going way back."

"You okay with that?"

"Yeah."

She nodded.

"I wasn't able to grasp it at first. You know, it's a little—out there?"

"A little?" she laughed. "You know, Ann. You're doing a great job adjusting. It's a lot to take in."

"I'll be fine. Now, on with your story." I rubbed my hands together.

"I'll start with the Seers. Before the Jacks wiped them out, they had predicted a great war." She took in a large breath and let it out. "The Seers knew they would die; they saw it."

I shuddered. "That would be horrible."

"It was. They also foretold a great battle between the Jacks and Readers. But they were unable to see who won, because there was an element that would decide the future of either group." She got up from the couch and asked, "Do you want some tea?"

"Now? Just when it's getting good?"

"I can make tea and talk at the same time." She opened an overhead cabinet. "Okay . . . where was I?" She poured the hot water into two mugs and grabbed a couple tea bags.

"You said an unknown element would decide when the war begins and how it ends." I sat on the stool in front of the kitchen bar.

"Yes. I should have said person. A person would be the deciding factor." After the tea bags were dunked a few times, she slid the mug across the counter.

"Who?" I took a small sip.

"The Seers called the person the Lost One. Whoever it was, male or female, had been whisked off thousands of years ago. The Seers could only envision a person who would save either group, but they don't know how they'd help specifically, only that whichever group had the Lost One would survive. So, you can imagine . . . we've been searching."

"I would think that person is quite valuable. Is it possible they're dead?"

"There's no way to know. I think a lot of people have given up—especially Archer and Devon." She pushed a bowl toward me. "Cream or sugar?"

"No, thanks. Why those two?"

"Well, the Seers said the four of us—me, Devon, Archer, and Markus—oh, you haven't met Markus yet. Anyway, the Lost One is the Soul Mate to one of us." She sighed. "It's so romantic."

"Wait. What do you mean, Soul Mate?"

"Destiny. Love. Forever. You know." She smiled and let out a sigh.

"Is that why Susie said Devon and Archer were like royalty?"

"Probably. It's put a bit of pressure on all of us. People sometimes treat us like we're different. Not in a bad way, but the expectations are high."

"How will you find the Lost One? I assume you don't know what they look like." I'd think, even if they were alive, they'd be impossible to identify and locate.

"Yes, they were vague on that. They said they'd find each other through touch. So, every time we find a new Reader, we fall all over ourselves to touch them." She shook her head and laughed. "It can be a little disconcerting to a new Reader. I'm sure they man-handled you when they first found you." She lifted an eyebrow.

"Not really. Um, what happens with the touch thing

anyway?" I rubbed the back of my neck.

"We've had a few false alarms. For some reason, Devon and Markus seem to set off sparks with some of the new Readers. But it has to be reciprocal."

Thank God. So my reaction to Devon was somewhat normal.

"How does Susie fit in with all this?" I asked.

"She's the one who's been telling everyone to give up—that we would have found this person by now. She's pretty much convinced everyone except for a few who still hold out hope." She picked up her cup of tea. "Come on, let's go back to the couch for the next part."

I followed her and burrowed into the corner, placing pillows on each side.

"All four of us haven't gotten serious with anyone because of the vision. We're waiting." She sighed. "But Susie has led an all-out campaign to win over either Devon or Archer. She thinks, because they flirt with her, she's making progress. But, to be honest, I think it's more of a game to them."

"Do they know that she's awful?" I slapped my hand over my mouth. "I don't know what's wrong with me lately. I seem to have lost my filter."

"Men. They're clueless. They think she's sweet." She stuck her tongue out and pretended to gag.

"So, let's recap. Before the Jacks killed the Seers, they predicted their demise and a big battle between the Readers and Jacks. The Lost One would be the deciding factor on which side would win."

She nodded.

"And there is a lost Reader who everyone is looking for."

"Well, that's not quite right. The Lost One is a mix of all three races. Whoever it turns out to be, they'll be able to read minds, implant their thoughts into others, and see the future."

"Really? Well, that makes things interesting. So, that's why the war could go either way. Is that right?" I asked.

"Exactly." She nodded. "It's hard to imagine one person having all that power. We could lose everything . . . including our lives."

"Would it be better if they were never found?"

"No." She let out a deep breath. "That would mean the Jacks would be able to keep up their campaign against humanity."

"What are they doing?"

"Well, they—" She slapped her hand over her mouth. "Oops. I've already said too much."

# CHAPTER II

"I'VE BEEN HERE A week; I think I can handle it." Doc finished my exam. I sat on the table with my legs swinging below. "That was tricky of you to delay the installation of the mirror after you found out, but I think it's time. I'm tired of looking at my reflection in the water and every glass door I see." I smiled to let him know I wasn't really angry. But this taking-it-slow idea was driving me nuts.

"Your arm looks great. It's almost healed. You've got the go-ahead for light physical activity." He gave my hand a gentle squeeze.

"Oh no, you don't. I know an avoidance technique when I hear one."

"It might be best to wait another week."

I shook my head.

"How stubborn are you going to be about this?"

"Very. I'll resort to any means possible." I pressed my lips together, but a small smile slipped past.

"You sure? You haven't regained any of your memory yet, so this could be a huge shock."

"Don't tell anyone, but I shined my stainless steel appliances to get a peek."

He threw his hands up. "I give up. Let me go find one." He went in the adjoining office.

Now that I'd talked him into it, hesitation took hold. It couldn't be that bad, *right?* Or maybe it could. Spending the last week with the best-looking people on the planet made me wonder how I'd measure up. Was I a troll in comparison? Could that be why they resisted letting me see myself?

Doc came back into the room with a plastic case clutched to his side. "If you're ready."

"I am."

He handed me the mirror. The overhead lights reflected off its surface. I slowly brought it up and took a peek.

An unfamiliar face stared back at me. I put the mirror down. *Okay.* I could handle this.

I started to bring it back up when Doc grabbed my arm. "You don't have to do this now."

"No, I'm okay." With my heart pounding, I lifted it up again and really looked. The breath I'd been holding came out in a big rush. "Thank God! I'm normal. I look like a normal girl."

Doc cocked an eyebrow. "You think you're normal looking?"

"Yes!" I giggled. "Wonderfully, ordinary. Brown hair, freckles, and all."

"Beauty is in the eye of the beholder, I guess." He smiled and added, "Most would call you extraordinary. But I won't argue with you if you're happy about it."

"So happy. The suspense has been killing me. Now I don't

have to worry about it anymore." Relief swept through me. My shoulders relaxed, and I unclenched my hands. I hadn't realized I'd been so anxious about it.

I jumped off the table and grabbed my sweater. "Can we lift the information ban now? How about classes? Can I start those?"

"Whoa. Hold up for a minute. Just because you passed the mirror hurdle, doesn't mean I want to bombard you with everything else. Remember, slow but sure is our motto."

My shoulders slumped. "Maybe just a class or two? The history one sounds interesting."

"You want more information about the Jacks."

"Sure do."

"Okay."

"Okay? That's it? No arm wrestling or anything?" I put on my sweater and pulled my hair free. "I could probably beat you, you fixed me up well." I flexed my arm to prove my point.

He laughed. "Not necessary. I'll let Lucy know you have clearance." He paused. "Lucy told me, or rather confessed, that she let you know a little of our history."

I nodded. "Yes, it's all very interesting."

"We haven't ruled you out yet."

"You mean as the Lost One? That's ridiculous. We'd know by now, right?"

"Not really. We don't know how far this touch thing goes, if you know what I mean." He fixed his collar on his shirt and shifted a little.

Oh, Doc was cute when nervous. "What do you mean exactly?"

"Archer and Devon have already touched you to see if

anything happened. You know, like angels singing or something like that." He chuckled. "Archer said if he were able to kiss you he was sure the angels would sing. But he also acknowledged it was too soon for you."

"It is too soon. What about Devon?"

"Devon? He's a hard nut to crack. He tells me he has no interest, but his eyes say otherwise."

No interest. Figures. *Jerk.*

"The true test will come next month. You'll meet Markus. He's coming back from his stint in India." He put his stethoscope away. "He's our last hope."

"For me? Why all this interest in me?"

"We scrutinize everyone we find. There's always a buzz of excitement in the compound when we discover a new Reader. But after we rule them out, it can be a little disheartening. Lucy probably told you we've been searching for a millennia. Now, we're dealing with three possibilities—one, the Lost One died during the war and subsequent wipe-out of the Seers, or even some time after. Two, the Jacks already have him or her." His face paled. "Three, we haven't found him or her yet. After thousands of years, we've almost given up." He stared at his desk. "I'd hoped it was you."

"I'm so sorry, Doc. I wish I could help." Thank God it wasn't me. That was a lot of responsibility for one soul to carry.

*You haven't met Markus yet.*

# CHAPTER 12

SLOW AND SURE WERE two words I could live without. It had been over a month since my arrival, yet the information still trickled in. Once in a while, a small detail would slip past someone who forgot I was still on a "need to know" basis— like, where the bathrooms were. *Grrr*. The biggest leak, thanks to Lucy's lapse, was when she referred to another compound in Colorado.

"Well?" I said, but she flushed pink and shook her head. Too late, though, I had already obtained some new information.

The few history classes I attended were interesting, but they hadn't given me much on the Jacks. The teacher, Ms. Hubbard, watered down most of the details. How to get more answers from her?

"Did the Jacks have anything to do with Hitler?" I asked. A hush went around the room. Ms. Hubbard's shoulders straightened and her lips pressed together.

Lucy nudged me and whispered, "You know she won't tell

you."

"Sshh. You never know when the dam will break."

Lucy was right, of course. Tight-lipped Ms. Hubbard gave a shake of her gray head. One of the Elders wouldn't make a mistake. I should have known.

"Maybe, one day, Betty will tell all." I giggled.

"Give it up, that woman is like Fort Knox." She put her books into a bag.

"What's Fort Knox?" I asked.

"I keep forgetting you don't know some of the most basic info." She grasped my hand and said, "That sounded bad. I didn't mean to imply . . ."

"I know." Lucy didn't have a mean bone in her body. She remained polite and kind to everyone, helped out when needed, and always remained upbeat. A real sweetheart. "It's okay. I know enough to get by."

"You'll learn a lot in your next class on self-defense. Doc's cleared you for the Kubotan instruction. Devon will be your teacher; he's the master." She eyed me, but I gave no reaction.

"Do I get to hit him in this class? Because that would be fun." I laughed.

"Yes! You can take out all your frustration on him." She giggled and added in a low voice, "I love having you here. I was about to die of boredom with the same people day after day. You, though, I'll never get tired of you."

"Aw. Really?"

She elbowed me. "Yes, really."

"You know what? I feel the same." Our connection was a warmth my spirit understood regardless of the memory loss. My ability to love was still intact.

"I know," she said, and we both stifled a laugh, not wanting to bring on the ire of Ms. Hubbard.

After class ended, we headed toward the gym. Trepidation no longer filled me as I led the way through the twisty corridors. I had this.

"When's the next escape drill? There hasn't been one since I arrived."

Lucy slowed her pace. "Honestly? I think the Elders thought you might run off or something."

"Why would they think that?" Did that mean I was a prisoner after all? The walls suddenly seemed closer together, the hallway shorter.

"They said it was because of your amnesia and considered it as possibility that you might become confused on the outside and make a dash for it. Their worst fear is you could be the Lost One and slip through our fingers." She motioned into an empty classroom. "Let's go in here."

"Are you going to tell me something I don't want to hear?"

"No, the opposite. I just wanted to let you know, if you ever want to go out, you know, into public, I'll take you myself."

Relief calmed my racing heart. "Thank you. My claustrophobia was about to make a return visit."

"We can go on a field trip. The Space Needle in Seattle is fun." She paused. "We'll have to start slow for your first few trips. Mind-reading can be upsetting at first."

"If I even am a mind-reader."

She grabbed my hand. "You are; I can feel it. Now, let's get going. We have to give Devon a smack-down."

"Yeah, right." I rolled my eyes. Devon had a lean, muscular frame and stood about a foot taller. At six-four, he could flatten me with his left pinky. Formidable in jeans and a t-shirt, I could only imagine what he'd be like all decked out in his Kubotan fighting clothes.

Mats were spread throughout the open room, ready for the class. We entered the gym, and, sure enough, Devon stood in front of the workout machines, looking intimidating with his scowl and tight-fitting, black, fighting clothes. Out of my element, I considered leaving.

His eyes darted to the wall clock. "You're late."

"Lighten up. I needed to talk to Ann about a few things." Lucy glared at her cranky brother.

"What things?"

"None-of-your-business-type things," I blurted out.

He turned toward me, eyes fierce, and asked, "Is that right?"

With hands on hips, faking bravado, I said, "Yes, that's right."

"We'll see how cocky you are after instruction." He continued to keep his laser stare locked on me.

"Okay, everyone. Let's get started." Archer clapped his hands, getting everyone's attention.

I hadn't noticed him with the distraction of His Darkness. Great, six people will get to watch me being flattened into a short stack.

"This is an advanced class, but we'll go slow for you," Devon said, folding his arms and leaning back against the weight machine.

I'd have given anything to wipe the condescending look from his face.

Archer came and stood next to me. "I can go over the basics

with her."

I almost kissed him.

"No. I'm the certified instructor. It's my job to get her started." Devon turned to address the class of six. "By now, you all know about the Kubotan, the stick we use for self-defense."

Lucy whispered in my ear, "It's small and it looks like a keychain. We keep it with us whenever we're on the outside."

Devon held out his palm, revealing a small, carved stick about six-and-a-half inches long. The ridges fit between each finger with the end coming to a point. "The Kubotan is a pressure point device. We use it for attacks in the fleshy and nerve targets. It's an effective tactic to get out of a close-quarters situation." He reached into a bag, pulled out a handful of matching sticks, and passed them out to everyone but me.

I held out my hand.

"You'll just watch today. These can be dangerous if you don't know what you're doing."

Yeah, like if I poked it in his big mouth.

"You can all get started." He turned to me. "Except for you."

He walked around the room, making sure the participants had the correct posture and attack moves.

Lucy paired with Archer, and it appeared they were evenly matched. Almost like a dance, they lunged and dipped, avoiding the weapon. I clapped my hands, rooting her on. Uh oh, that happened quickly. Archer had her on the floor with the weapon at her neck. He smiled and offered a hand up. Lucy brushed herself off, and they started again.

Bored after thirty minutes, I decided to try to get in on the fun. I called across the room, "Hey, Devon? I'd like to hold the

Kubotan to get the feel of it. Unless, of course, you think I might hurt you?"

Lucy and Archer snickered, but stopped when Devon shot them a death glare.

"You want a lesson?" His hands tightened around the weapon.

"Yes?" My confidence from a minute ago had left the building.

He walked over and stood in front of me. "Put out your hand."

*Please, oh please, don't let my hand tremble.* I stretched it out with my palm up, my hand staying steady. What a relief. "I'm ready."

He placed the Kubotan in the center of my palm, and it felt . . . nice. I wrapped my fingers around it. Warm, of course, Devon held it throughout the class, but there was also a weird vibration. I tightened my grip and let the sensations travel up my arm. The same feelings from the beach came whooshing back—oh no, that couldn't be right. I dropped it on the floor, the sound making a pinging noise as it bounced from me back to Devon. All activity stopped.

Devon smirked. "You don't have to be afraid of it."

Something inside me snapped, and blinding, white-hot anger took over. Not afraid or intimidated anymore, I picked up the Kubotan and said, "Come at me."

Devon held up his hands. "I'm not going to hurt you. Just because your pride—"

"I said, come take this weapon."

"When I take it, will you follow directions from now on? You'll listen? I know what I'm doing."

"You have a deal. If you can get this Kubotan from me, I'll follow every instruction."

His arrogant smile was back. If the powerful tingling, surging through every cell in my body, was an indication of this outcome, his smile would be short-lived.

Devon circled around me. I envisioned his every move, focusing on my defense.

He didn't have a chance.

How did I know this? No matter, I kept my attention on his slow perusal. I stood still, turning only when he moved out of sight.

He would try to maneuver a right wrist hold to force the Kubotan out of my hand. The simplest move, without a risk of injury. He lunged, going for my wrist. I rotated it so my thumb lined up with his, bent sharply, and pulled away, moving a few feet back. "Aw, you can do better than that, can't you?" I didn't know what had come over me, but I couldn't stop.

His eyes narrowed. "Lucky move."

My size, weight, or strength didn't matter. The laws of physics were on my side. Strategy was all I needed.

Again, I anticipated each move. A bear hug from behind would be next. I let him grab me, putting his arms around my middle. Autopilot kicked in. I stomped his foot while grabbing one arm, and, with my other arm, elbowed him in the nose. He hesitated for half a second, and I took advantage, landing a roundhouse kick to his kneecap. He yelped and landed on the floor, wheezing with a bloody nose and an injured leg.

Oh no. What had I done?

"I'm so sorry! I don't know what came over me. Are you hurt?"

He tried to get up, but lay back down. He wiped his bloody

nose with his shirt then smiled.

*What?*

"You get to keep the Kubotan. I'm pretty sure you know how to use it." He groaned. "Is everyone just going to stand there?"

Archer and Caleb, another student, grabbed each arm and pulled him up. He steadied himself and winced a little when he tried to put weight on his left leg.

"You'll need an x-ray," Archer said.

"No, it's not broken. The muscle is just bruised. I'll be fine." He continued to wipe the blood from his nose with his t-shirt.

"Anything else bruised?" Archer laughed, which earned him a fixed stare from Devon.

"Go ahead. You take her on and see what happens."

"No, thank you. I've seen enough." Archer turned and asked, "How long have you known about your ability? Were you saving it so you'd have some fun?"

"No." I pushed the hair from my face. "I didn't know anything until the Kubotan was in my hand." I kept my expression blank, but inwardly did a happy dance and victory cheer.

"Interesting. What do you think, Archer?" Devon asked.

"It must have triggered a memory. Or unleashed superhuman powers." He chuckled. "I never thought I'd see the day when anyone took you down. Especially a girl like Ann."

"Hey," I said.

"Oh, sorry, Ann." Archer continued to laugh.

Lucy put her arm around my shoulder. "Well, I'm proud of her. But she looks like she could sleep for a few days. Let's go back to your room and order pizza from the kitchen."

"Sounds great." I turned to get my bag.

"Wait." Devon limped toward me and reached out his hand, his eyes locked on mine. "No hard feelings."

The only times we'd touched were on the beach and just now during the fight, both uncomfortable with the same warm and tingly sensation. Today, I hoped it had more to do with the Kubotan weapon. If it wasn't . . . No, it couldn't be. I hesitated. He cocked his eyebrow and tilted his head. Would he be able to tell I was possibly one of his groupie Readers who got all sparky when he touched me?

Not wanting to give him the satisfaction, I grabbed his hand and gave it a good shake. "Thank you for the . . . instruction." I dropped it quickly, grabbed Lucy by the arm, and marched out of the gym. "Let's go."

Once in the hallway, my head spun, and I became short of breath. This wasn't the warm tingles from before. More like I'd been in a steam room for hours. My skin burned hot, and a frenetic sparking sensation started at my hand and worked its way through my body.

"Ann! You're red as a beet. Are you all right?" Lucy's worried gaze traveled over my face.

"I think I'm having a delayed reaction to the fight." I fanned myself hoping to cool down.

"We're going to see Doc." She tugged my arm in the opposite direction.

"No!" I pulled free. "All I need is a cold shower. Really, I'll be fine."

"If you aren't your usual white self after the shower, I'm calling Doc. Okay?"

"It's a deal." It better work. How would I explain this? *Dear*

*God, let the shower take this burning feeling away.* I didn't want to get their hopes up that I had some sort of soul mate thing going on with Devon. Sure, he was gorgeous beyond belief, and funny when he wanted to be. He loved his sister, even though she drove him crazy, which was kind of sweet. But I also found him irritating and impossible, infuriating and stubborn. I didn't have any feelings for him. None. Not at all.

After returning to my room, Lucy took over. "You," she pointed down the hallway, "get in the shower. Don't come out until you're a light pink. I'll call for the pizza. What do you want to drink?"

"Tea, maybe?"

"I can do that. Get going." She gave me a gentle push.

A loud knocking at the door interrupted us. "What now?" I groaned.

Lucy approached the door and looked through the peephole. "You're going to love this." She opened the door and there stood Susie.

Could this day get any worse?

# CHAPTER 13

" SUSIE, UH, WHAT ARE you doing here?" I asked.

She stepped inside, and her eyes traveled up and down my body. "Why are you so red? What's wrong with you?"

Ugh. "Nothing. I'm just a little overheated. I'm on my way to the shower. Can I help you with something?"

"Yes, you can. I, uh, came to ask you a question." She tucked her picture-perfect, glossy hair behind one ear. "I'm having a party tomorrow night, and I wanted you to come." She said it so fast, I almost didn't understand the words.

Lucy asked, "Who? Both of us?"

"Yes. Both of you. I want you both to come. Eight o'clock in the Hub. It's my birthday. It's for me. Okay. Good-bye." She turned and walked out the door.

"That was weird," I said.

"So strange."

We both stared at the door.

"I wonder if Archer or Devon had anything to do with this," I asked. It was hard to imagine Susie would want me anywhere near her birthday party.

Lucy snapped her fingers. "Of course! That's it."

"Should we go?"

"Oh, yeah. It's bound to be a spectacle."

Twenty-four hours later and there I sat while Lucy prepared me for Susie's party. With my skin color back to normal, all systems were go. Now I just needed Lucy to back off.

"I don't need any more make-up," I said, swatting her hand away.

"Wait. I'm almost done. It's called the smoky eye. You're going to knock 'em dead."

"Someone's going to die if they don't get their hands off me."

"Just one more swipe and I'll be done."

"One swipe? You said that ten minutes ago." Nothing short of a powerhouse, Lucy couldn't be stopped once something lodged in her brain, so I gave up and let her continue. She finished working on my eyes and stood back to admire her artistry.

"Your eyes . . . I can't believe how beautiful they are. I wish mine were bright blue and oval like yours." She handed me a mirror. "What do you think?"

"A raccoon?"

"Oh, stop it." She nudged my shoulder. "Now, we'll need the perfect dress."

"Can't I wear my usual t-shirt and jeans?"

"This is a party. Haven't you . . . Never mind. No, you can't wear casual. Birthday parties are a big thing around here. Everyone gets dressed up, and there'll be dinner and dancing. You'll love it."

"Dancing? Will there be a band?"

"No. They usually pipe in music from a pre-recording. Susie loves the fifties, so we'll probably have to listen to doo-wop all night," she said, rolling her eyes.

"I like that music. Oh, no. Do you think I'll have to be friends with Susie now?" I laughed.

"No, but I think I'll need to broaden your music base. Have you listened to any grunge rock yet?"

"Not yet. My music appreciation class has only made it to the sixties. I really like the Beatles."

She shook her head. "I'll need to skip you ahead to the Nirvana years. Anyway, plenty of time for that. For now, let's find you the perfect dress."

Lucy stood before a line-up of party dresses in my closet. She whipped through and grabbed a little black swatch of fabric.

"This one." She grinned with a glint in her eye.

"What size is that? It looks like an eight-year-old would need to squeeze into it."

"It's made for you. You'll look stunning. Now get out of those sweats, and let's get this party started."

A few minutes later, stuffed into a tight-fitting, black dress, we prepared to leave for the party. "Are you sure this isn't too tight?" I pulled the fabric up to cover my chest then pulled it down to cover more of my legs.

"It's just right, take my word for it."

"And these heels, I think I might fall off them. How about some flats?"

"Did you or did you not ask me to help you?" She crossed her arms and waited.

Did I? What was I thinking?

"Yes. But—"

"No buts. I'm your stylist for the evening. Trust me, the men won't know what hit them."

"Your dress isn't as short. How about we switch? This black number would look terrific with your skin. Have I told you how beautiful you look?"

"Flatterer. Don't try to sweet talk me out of the dress. Now come on." She pulled me out the door before I could argue anymore. Halfway down the first hall, I wobbled on my heels.

"You're going to need more practice. We'll take the long way to the Hub," she said.

"Won't that make us late?" The last thing I wanted to do was give Susie another reason to hate me.

"I have a feeling Susie didn't even want us to come. So, no, we can take our time."

"That's probably true. Can you give me some tips? How do I walk in these things?"

"All you have to do is—"

"Hey, girls." Archer came from around the corner. "I was looking for you." He stopped mid-step and gasped. "You look, you look . . . I'm speechless."

"You can thank me." Lucy bowed. "I'm the artist and Ann the canvas."

Devon joined our small group and asked Lucy, "What did you do to her?"

"Isn't it obvious? I curled her hair, applied make-up—"

"That's not what I'm talking about and you know it. She can't go out in public looking like that."

A sudden coldness hit my core. "Like what?" I asked and shot my iciest stare at him.

"Things are . . . things are showing," he said as his hand swept up and down.

"Yes, she has legs. Get over it." Lucy hooked her arm in mine. "Now, if you'll excuse us, we have a party to get to."

With my head held high, we left the two standing in the hallway. Archer shouted, "I think you look great, Ann."

Without turning, I waved, wishing I could disappear.

We stepped around the corner, and I pulled at the clingy fabric. "I told you this was too short."

"Don't listen to Devon. He's been acting weird lately."

"How so?"

"Moody. Well, moodier than usual I should say. He also seems distracted a lot." She stopped and lowered her voice. "You don't feel anything for him, do you?"

"What? I mean, no. Well, I do feel irritation if that counts."

*Liar.*

She laughed. "You're going to have to get past your irritation before you kiss him."

"Wait. What do you mean, kiss him? I'm not going to kiss him."

"Devon, Markus, Archer, and I have to kiss all the new Readers. You didn't know that? It's no big deal. The Elders want to be able to rule out the soul mate thing. Just in case."

"They can't make me, can they?" I held my hands together

in an attempt to hide the trembling.

"No, of course not. But aren't you curious? I've kissed plenty of new Readers over the years. Just a quick peck on the lips is all that's needed. Easy." She shrugged.

Devon's lips were full and soft looking. I didn't think a kiss with him would be quick *or* easy.

Uh oh. I wanted to kiss Devon.

"Your face is doing that flushing thing again. Don't worry, you can wait as long as you like. Once, in the nineteen-twenties, I made a Reader wait for two years."

"Why?" That seemed like a long time.

"Adam was pompous and arrogant." She giggled. "And those were his best qualities. Yeah, he needed to be taken down a notch or two. I'll point him out to you next time I see him."

"Sounds familiar." I winked, half-joking.

"Devon does seem that way on the surface. But he's really great when he lets down his guard." Her face softened. "I wouldn't mind, you know, if you decided to pursue things."

"With Devon? Uh-uh. He disapproves of everything I do. You saw him earlier."

"Yeah. His reaction was interesting. Either he thinks of you as a sister, or . . . something else. It'll be fun to see which." We stood outside the door to the Hub. "All ready?"

"No." I laughed.

She gave my hand a little tug and pulled me inside.

"Holy cow."

I expected a 1950s theme with a jukebox, poodle skirts, and Hula Hoops . . . but, instead, we were greeted with a simple elegance. White linen cloths draped over the wood tables, china plates, and sparkling silverware transformed the room. A crystal vase with a single rose sat in the middle of each table. Apparently, Susie went for a different type of fifties atmosphere.

Around a hundred Readers were clustered in small groups, talking and laughing, their voices mingling with the Frank Sinatra tune floating from the speakers. Twinkling lights were strung, crisscrossing around the ceiling, casting a warm and festive glow around the room.

"Nice, isn't it?" Archer asked.

I jumped back. "Where did you come from?"

"I told you; I'm always watching your back." He smiled and took a step closer.

"You'll want to be careful tonight, Ann," Devon warned.

They were a team, but did they always have to be together?

"Why is that?"

"We're Readers, not angels," Devon said as his eyes scanned me again.

"I can protect myself, remember?" I pretended to crack my knuckles and grinned. It earned me a half-smile.

"Yeah. I still have the limp." This time, I was assaulted by his full smile. Something small and annoying fluttered in my stomach.

*Stop that.*

"Come on. Let's grab a table and order some appetizers from the waiters." Lucy beckoned us to a table close to the dance floor.

"Waiters? Since when?" I asked.

"We all volunteer for birthday parties, anniversaries, weddings—any kind of celebration. I have a shift next month.

You should come and do it with me. We get to wear uniforms and everything."

I smiled. Every day, I fell more in love with my new home. A sense of belonging replaced the ache of loneliness. The emptiness had become manageable now because of this small community I'd come to trust.

I sat at the table with Lucy and studied the menu.

"May I have this dance?" Archer stretched out his hand.

"Oh. I didn't expect . . . I mean, I'm not prepared." This didn't fit my plan to politely decline any type of dancing tonight. First, I didn't know how. Second, because of the deadly contraptions called heels Lucy coaxed me to wear. I had to fess up. "Dancing and me, well, we don't mix well."

"It doesn't matter. I'll teach you."

With the expectant little-boy expression on his face, I didn't have the heart to say no.

"I'll try, but don't blame me if I step on your toes."

"I welcome it."

His black-tie suit was tailored to show off his trimmed and toned body. His hair was a little messy, with his blonder streaks interweaved with the darker shades and textures, making him look like he'd just come off a tropical beach. He spent a lot of time in the greenhouse, turning his skin a smooth, golden brown. Handsome was not an adequate word to describe him.

Every time I was pulled toward Devon, Archer would say or do something that would draw me away. His timing was spot-on.

"You have yourself a dance partner." I let him tug me out of the chair and lead me to the center of the raised dance floor. He nodded to the DJ, and another song began to play. "This is nice. Who is it?" I asked.

"You should be learning about Nat King Cole in your music class. It released in the early 1950s. Have you listened to his music?" He stepped closer.

"Not yet. But I love this song so far."

Archer pulled me into his arms and placed his warm hand on my back. "Just lean into me, and I'll show you what to do."

I took his advice. His hold on my back tightened, and he bent down a little and sang along with the song, "Unforgettable, that's what you are."

Goosebumps popped up along my arms and legs. He continued to sway me to the music while he sang softly in my ear. Oh, this was nice, and he smelled so good. Like fresh linens and a light cologne.

Were goosebumps similar to tingles? For the sake of avoiding complications—well, Devon, and his disapproving looks and moodiness—I hoped I'd bond with anyone except him.

*Please, oh, please let it be Archer.* He always made me laugh and stayed out of the "friend" or "brother" category with his gentle touches during class or his ability to stop any alone time I might have with Devon.

Archer pressed against me even closer and whispered, "I want to kiss you, Ann. No, I take that back. I *need* to kiss you. I'm dying here." He continued to run his hands up and down my back, creating a firestorm of emotions.

Warmth turned to red-hot heat. My fingers clutched the back of his coat, pulling.

"We'll have to kiss sooner or later for the Elders, so why not sooner?" he asked.

I smiled. "So, let me get this straight. You want to kiss me for a bunch of old people?"

"No. It's because I feel . . ." Now his lips were on my neck, barely brushing back and forth. If he didn't stop, I might do something foolish, like kiss him in front of everyone at the party.

He bent his knees so we were eye-to-eye, so close I smelled the minty toothpaste on his breath. His eyes glanced down at my lips and lifted back up, searching for my response. I nodded once.

Devon tapped on Archer's arm. "The song has ended." How did he do that, always show up at the most awkward moments?

Archer sighed and dropped his head on my shoulder. He groaned. "So close." We both laughed.

He took my hand and led us back to the table. I sat next to Lucy, who clasped my hand under the table. "What the . . . what was that?"

"What?" I asked, making sure my expression was the picture of innocence.

"Archer. You know what I'm talking about." She moved closer. "Devon looked like he'd blow a gasket. I've ruled out brotherly feelings."

A screeching noise from the speakers interrupted her interrogation.

"That noise." I covered my ears.

"I don't kn—"

*This is USA Radio Network. This broadcast is brought to you by USA Network, Seattle, bringing you the headlines from the US and the World. I'm Steven Bishop, and here are today's top stories.*

Lucy took a firm hold of my arm. "Let's go."

"Wait. What's going on?"

*"Police have released new information on the Ann Baker Case, the eighteen-year-old wanted for the murder of her parents, Don & Laurin Baker. Ms. Baker was believed dead after diving into the cold waters of Elliott Bay after being shot by Seattle Police. A remnant of clothing retrieved from Lopez Island, part of the San Juan Islands, revealed matching DNA . . ."*

My head felt light, and my heart beat so fast, I was sure it would burst.

"Lucy." I rubbed my arm where the bullet wound had healed. "The police shot me? I thought maybe the Jacks had. Why didn't you tell me? Is this why I'm not allowed out? Everyone here believes I'm a murderer?"

"No. No." Tears welled in Lucy's eyes. "I'm sorry. I wanted to tell you."

"It's true?" Betrayal clawed and ripped through the shock. I looked around the room. The party atmosphere had come to a complete halt. Every pair of eyes were on me. Everyone knew.

I got up from the table. The fury, disappointment, sadness, and, finally—loneliness were staggering. My emotions were so excruciating, my chest squeezed where my heart pounded. Painful enough to kill me, or at least, strong enough to make me want to die. Nothing here was real. Too many half-truths and lies. "I'm going to the bathroom. I need a few minutes."

"I'll go with you." Lucy stood next to me.

"Alone. I need to go alone. Can you give me a few minutes, please?"

She fidgeted with the hem on her dress and muttered, "Okay. But don't be long. We need to talk about this."

I left the room. Another flash of my parents smiling faces

came and left before I could grab onto the memory. If they wouldn't give me the answers I needed, I'd get them myself.

One thing I knew for sure. I didn't kill my parents, but I'd find out who did. But I couldn't do it from inside the compound.

They want to shut me out of my own life? Well, think again.

I would break out of this place, and no one could stop me.

# CHAPTER 14

HOW LONG WOULD IT be before they noticed my disappearance? I kicked off my heels and chucked them in a garbage can on the way back to my room. My hands grabbed onto the delicate fabric of my dress, and I yanked it off over my head. I stepped into my closet, picking up and tossing the needed items onto my bed. After slipping on jeans and a t-shirt, I pulled my book bag off the floor. I dumped the contents and packed two pairs of jeans, sweaters, a warm jacket, underwear, toiletries, and an extra pair of comfortable shoes.

I stopped. My books. I ran my finger over their smooth surface, already missing the life I thought I had. The life I wanted.

*Quit waiting around. Find the truth.*

With the bag over my shoulder, I grabbed a knife and flashlight from the kitchen drawer, stuffing them in with my other supplies.

How to get out of the compound? Ugh. I headed out my

door, clueless. *Think*. Perhaps I could hide in the back of a delivery truck? But all the truck drivers were Readers, so they might recognize me. Nope. That won't work.

Lucy . . . laundry.

The vents.

Lucy hated laundry duty and would often drag me along. I reversed my direction and doubled my speed to the west side of the compound. The laundry room had big vents that had to go somewhere. It was one of the few places I had access.

The blood in my veins rushed so hard, it reverberated in my ears, making it difficult to hear anything around me. I practiced deep breathing, hoping to appear relaxed in case I passed anyone in the corridor.

I made it to the laundry room, placed my hand on the entry pad, and prayed. If access was denied, that would mean one thing—they knew of my plans. The door clicked open, and I sighed in relief. My eyes scanned around the room. Empty. I headed toward the dryers. Sure enough, huge industrial tubes, attached to the back of the dryers, went into a wall leading who knew where, but I was about to find out.

I squeezed behind the large dryer and pulled on the tube. It was stuck on with a few screws and a metal ring. The knife shook as I pressed and turned firmly to remove the screws. I tugged it free. Wow. This was going to be a tight squeeze, but doable.

The laundry room door squeaked open and closed. "Ann's not going to be in here. What, she's going to fold her clothes before making a big escape?" Becca from my art history class asked, standing only a few feet from my hiding place.

I prayed they wouldn't see me. Beads of sweat dampened my forehead.

"I know. I mean, why would she leave Samara? She'd have

the cops and Jacks all over her. It's not safe," a male voice I didn't recognize said.

"Yeah, you're right. She wouldn't leave. She's probably in one of the classrooms, wanting to be alone. I'll bet it was hard for her to find out her parents were murdered like that." They left the room, and the door clicked shut behind them.

The police and Jacks waited for me on the outside. I paused, looking at my escape tube. What was the alternative? My desire to know overpowered the temptation to go back to my warm, safe room.

For now, everyone would think I was off brooding on my own. But that wouldn't last. Back to the tube. Could I do this? What would happen if I became stuck? Or if I suffered a panic attack and passed out?

*Stop it. You can do this.*

I pushed my bag in first, took a deep calming breath, and crawled into the tube, still warm from the last load of clothes. By grabbing onto a metal ring every few feet, I was able to pull myself forward, working my way out of the main laundry area. The farther I went, the darker it became. My hand dug around my escape bag and landed on the flashlight. I flipped it on and illuminated the tube across a long corridor that would hopefully lead me out. Except, about twenty feet away, two red dots appeared . . .

*Eyes.*

My hand slapped over my mouth to muffle the scream that wanted to escape. Really? A rat, or mouse. The distinction didn't matter. The disgusting creature was here, with *me*.

I put my head against the cool metal duct. "Shoo," I hissed. Of course, he didn't leave.

If that rodent knew what was good for him, he'd hightail it out before my flashlight landed on him. My stomach turned.

"Go bye-bye, little mousey." I waved my flashlight at him. He stayed still, watching me. When I inched toward him, he finally skittered off.

Smart mouse.

I rounded the first corner, and a little bit of light cut through the darkness. Still moving forward, excitement replaced the dread and fear from a few minutes ago. I wiped my forehead with my shirt.

A lint filter was my last barrier. I gave it a good yank, and it loosened. A few more pushes and pulls and I had it out.

My bag went out the opening first. I crawled out and jumped down a three-foot drop. Freedom. I'd done it. I breathed in the cool, autumn air and tipped my head back, turning my face to the sky. The moon, bright and beautiful, gave me the needed light to move forward.

I brushed off my filthy jeans, and threw on my warm coat. I wasn't in the clear yet. The next hurdle would be the guard at the entrance.

I closed my eyes and brought back the map in my head of all the turns from the guard station to the compound. My other option was the cement wall with the thin wire running along the top that enclosed the entire neighborhood. Not wanting to find out what that wire was all about, I knew slipping past the guard at the main gate would be my best option.

I kept in a crouched position, darting in and out of the trees, avoiding all the houses until I made it to the guardhouse. The uniformed man inside leaned back in his chair, eating a sandwich.

No one knew I was out.

The phone rang, and he turned to answer it. This was my chance. I sprinted under his line of sight, out into the night.

I ran fast, all knees and elbows flying as an alarm went off. The clanking of the gates signaled their closure. My head turned as I searched for the best route. The roads would be too risky. I'd duck into the woods and wait until morning. Maybe they'd spend all night searching the houses. If that was the case, I had myself a good head start.

Stiffness and freezing cold temperatures greeted me upon first waking. Curled up into a ball with leaves piled over me to keep me warm hadn't worked. I stood up, stretched, and enjoyed the warmth of the morning sun.

Suddenly, realization struck. This was the first time I'd been alone since the beach. Completely alone. Tears stung my eyes. My fists tightened, and I dredged up the determination to move forward. Once I learned more about my parents and what had happened, maybe it would spark something.

I couldn't stop. I *wouldn't* stop. Not until I found the truth.

A plan was what I needed. First up—a disguise. If the police were looking for me, I wouldn't make their job easy. A grocery store should have hair color and scissors. Out here in North Bend, they most likely wouldn't be looking for a girl on the run.

I dodged through the woods, following the direction of the cars on the highway. After an exhausting two hours, I spied a little town next to the freeway. Before walking out from the safety of the forest, I checked for the Jeep Devon drove, but it was nowhere to be seen. With shoulders straight, I strode into the little grocery store like I owned the place.

*Wow. She's hot.*

A young clerk, about sixteen, sat at attention behind the checkout counter. "May I help you?" he asked.

*I'd do anything for you. I could be your love slave.*

My head veered back in his direction.

A wide grin spread across his face.

"What? What did you say?" This kid was a creep.

"I just asked if I could help you find anything?"

Oh, now he acts all innocent.

*Look at that bimbo flirting with the kid.*

I turned to see a forty-something woman with bleach-blond hair, staring at me.

"Who's the bimbo?" I asked her, seething.

She stared for a moment, eyes wide, and dropped her bag of flour.

After her startled look, comprehension struck. Uh oh. I must have heard her thoughts. And it must have been the kid's thoughts as well. My heart raced, and I broke into a sweat.

*I am a Reader after all.*

Keep it together.

"You—you." Her eyes widened. "You're the—" She ran from the store yelling, "Don't hurt me. Don't hurt me."

The media. Everyone believed I was some murderer.

"Do you really want to help me?" I asked the stunned kid.

He swallowed. "I have to go home. My mom's waiting for me."

*She's going to kill me now, I know it.*

Ugh. Just what I thought. Best to get on with it.

"Here come with me." I pulled him along. "I have to get some hair color. Where is it?"

He picked a box off the shelf.

"No, not blond. Grab the black. Never mind, I'll take both." Just in case he's questioned by police, I didn't want to tip them off.

"Oh, and where are the scissors?"

"Over here. Which ones?" He held up two.

"The larger pair. Now I just need water and some snacks"

"They're at the register."

"Perfect, because I'm going to need some money."

He winced, his body deflating.

"Don't worry, I'll return it all in a few days. Do you have a car?"

*Not my Mustang!*

"When I'm done with it, I'll drop it safe and sound at . . . the Space Needle. How about that?"

He dug in his pocket and pulled out a set of keys. Closing his eyes, he dropped them into my waiting hand.

Back in the parking lot, I threw the bag with the supplies on the passenger seat, got in, and peeled out. Poor kid. Oh well, he'd get over it, and have a good story to tell his friends. Once on the road, I let the store incident sink in. I *was* a Reader. They hadn't lied about everything. I took small comfort from that.

After a few blocks, I pulled over into a nice, safe-looking neighborhood. Not Seattle. Sorry, kid, the police would be on high alert. It was just the type of place where people would forget to lock their car doors.

Sure enough, after three tries, the door of a Ford Taurus opened. I pulled out my knife and removed the plastic panels covering the steering column. Crouching under the wheel, I examined the car's ignition lock, the ignition, and starter motor. A wiring diagram flashed into my head. I tugged loose the wires and prepared to connect them. First the dash lights came on, and, after the third wire was added, the car started.

How in the world did I know how to do this?

My getaway with the new car would only give me an hour, tops. The police would most likely find the Mustang and figure out another car had been stolen. To remain undetected, I'd need to repeat this at least three more times before I made it to Seattle.

Two hours, a haircut, color change, and three cars later, I parked in the lot of the Seattle Public Library.

I approached the librarian behind the counter. "Can I use one of the computers? I have some homework." I motioned to my backpack.

"You need a library card." She went back to her filing.

"Uh. I don't have one. My purse was stolen from my car yesterday, and they took everything." I blinked trying to look like I was holding back tears.

*Oh, that poor girl.*

"My dear, that's terrible. I'll get you a guest pass." She reached under the counter and handed it to me with a sympathetic smile.

"Thank you." I sniffed one more time for good measure. That wasn't so difficult.

Now I needed to find a computer away from people. I wouldn't be able to concentrate with a crowd of thoughts interfering.

Once I settled in and began reading through all the articles about my parents, I soon discovered it was harder than I thought. So many things twisted inside my gut. Memories I had repressed?

They were college professors, working together at North Seattle University. Their specialty was telekinesis and, no surprise, mind-reading.

*What were you trying to accomplish? And why did someone kill you?*

The articles about me read like a trashy gossip magazine, sensationalizing the murders and implying I had something to do with it. The police didn't have any concrete evidence against me. I almost groaned out loud when I read, '*The young and beautiful Ms. Baker had acted strangely during questioning.*' All they cared about was drama—selling more papers. Also, who wouldn't act off? My parents had just died. What did they expect? The big scandal was the fact I had disarmed a cop and escaped.

The next line stopped my breath.

*No.*

*Dr. Don Baker and Dr. Laurin Baker both perished in a house fire. The Fire Marshal deemed the fire suspicious, and has ordered an arson investigation.*

I closed my eyes and let the wave of emotion hit. Guilt clawed its way up my throat. Could I have saved them? Where was I during all this? I continued to flip through every news article available without gaining any more information.

Time to take action. I needed answers. We had lived on Capitol Hill, a residential neighborhood a few miles from the city center, according to one of the articles. My new destination.

The next two hours were spent driving down unfamiliar streets in the most eclectic neighborhood imaginable. On one street corner, a drug deal went down, on the next sat an expensive French restaurant. The houses also varied, from dilapidated to multi-million dollar mansions. I crossed over

Broadway Avenue into one of the oldest neighborhoods in Seattle.

At least, that's what the sign stated. The large homes were elegant with their columns and brick masonry. Huge front porches with rocking chairs and impeccable landscaping added to their beauty. I slowed and stopped in front of a house with a chain-link fence and crime tape hanging around the exterior. The house appeared vacant—dark. After closer inspection, black smoke stains up the west side of the house from the first floor reaching to the second confirmed it. This was it.

I put my head on the steering wheel and waited, half expecting my entire life to come rushing back.

Nothing. Not one single memory.

I'd need to get in the house somehow. Maybe if I touched the walls or found a personal item it would spark something. Anything. I scanned up and down the street for suspicious activity. I pulled the hoodie up over my head and got out of the truck.

A walk around the neighborhood would give me the opportunity to see if anyone or anything seemed out of place. I cleared my head, hoping to catch a thought or two, but it appeared my ability to mind-read only reached a few feet away. Probably a good thing.

I circled the block, decided it was safe, and approached the house from the back alley. I shimmied under a small opening in the fence, wiped off the dirt, and walked to the back door. My hand twisted the doorknob and found it open. Police. They were so sloppy.

Inside, the damp, stagnant air made the hairs in my nose burn, and I rubbed it, trying to rid myself of the sensation. Traces of smoke lingered, but the smell of mold overpowered it. Sections of ceiling hung loose, and plaster fragments littered the floor. I avoided them and moved into the kitchen area. It wasn't any better. Between the fire and the subsequent police investigation, everything was in shambles. Overturned chairs, cupboard doors left open, grease spots on the floor, and broken dishes cluttered the countertops.

Not everything was broken though. A mug with *Best Dad* in bold lettering sat undisturbed next to the sink. I picked it up, held it to my chest, and let the sadness sweep through me.

*Please let me remember them.*

"Too little, too late, Sweetcakes," a strange voice said.

I whipped around, still clutching the cup.

"Your memory won't come back for at least another year." He smirked. A big man, probably six-foot-five, stood by the door I'd just come through. His large, protruding stomach added to his already large frame.

"How would you know that? Who are you?"

"I'm just a guy. But now, I'll be a hero. We've been tracking you for centuries." He pulled a gun from his jacket. "Don't worry. I won't shoot unless you try to get away." With his other hand, he pulled out a phone, punched a number, and said, "I've got her."

"No, you don't."

Devon?

I turned to see him in the doorway on the other side of the kitchen.

I closed my eyes, the relief overwhelming. But when I opened them again, the other man was grinning.

"Well, well, well. The great Devon Dionysius. I never thought I'd see the day. Either she's the Lost One, or you *think* she is. You've taken a risk coming after her, and you failed." His smile remained smug.

Devon leaned against the counter. "No, she took something of mine when she left. Once I get it back, you can have her. She's useless to us."

What? I glared at Devon, but he kept his eyes on the other man.

His eyebrow rose. "Just like that?"

Devon crossed his arms. "Just like that."

# CHAPTER 15

MY MOUTH FELL OPEN, and I shook my head. If I were closer, I'd smash Devon with my flashlight like I'd planned to do with the rodent.

*For God's sake, if you can hear me, go along with it.*

I glanced over to the heavy-set man to see if he'd reacted to Devon's thought. He stared at me with one eyebrow raised. What a relief. He hadn't looked at Devon or heard his voice.

"So what? It's only a necklace." I rolled my eyes.

"That belonged to my mother," Devon said through gritted teeth. I'd have to congratulate him on his acting skills later. *If we got out of this mess.*

*Grab anything and use it like the Kubotan.*

Devon's thoughts distracted me, making it hard to keep the flow of conversation realistic. "I had to have something to pawn." I shrugged.

"No way. I can't believe it," said another gun-slinging mountain of a man who entered the kitchen. He stared at

Devon with wide eyes.

We were doomed.

"We should probably kneel before His Highness." He laughed and turned his three-hundred-pound-plus body to his partner. "What are we going to do with him?"

"We'll kill him, of course," the first man said in a bored voice.

"The Agreement?" Devon's hands curled into fists.

The first man waved him off. "That thing? It was written over two thousand years ago. It doesn't apply anymore. We've had a bounty on your head for years. Coming here, where you knew we'd be waiting, was a big mistake." He leered. "I don't know if I'm more excited to kill you, or to capture the girl."

They wanted to kill Devon? The fury that raged through my blood was so potent, every fiber came to attention. A picture of what I needed to do formed in my brain. Every move choreographed down to how many breaths I'd take.

"If you break The Agreement, there'll be war." Devon didn't take his eyes off the first man.

"Do you think we care? We'll win now that we have the Lost One." He shifted and grinned at his partner.

The huge man said in a low voice, "Maybe we shouldn't kill him yet. We need The Lost One. Devon doesn't seem too interested."

"Are you dim-witted? We have the girl; she's the one." He turned to me with a menacing grin. "You'll help us, won't you, Sweetcakes?"

"Help you? How am I supposed to help you when I don't even remember my own name?" I knew in that moment, all the people I'd come to care about were in grave danger. I shouldn't have run off on my own. *Stupid. Stupid.*

"A little truth serum and torture will rectify that." He pushed numbers into his cell. "We're ready. Pull the van into the back alley."

Time to put my plan into action. I picked up the bag at my feet.

Two guns aimed at my head.

Unafraid and in the zone, I asked, "What? I can't bring my things?"

"Put the bag on the table. Slowly," the first man instructed.

The table sat two feet from them. With my emotions now under control, power started to build inside me. I placed the bag on the table and slowly tipped it over. I held the knife through the fabric so it wouldn't fall out. The items would seem benign, but they wouldn't be for long.

I closed my eyes and focused. A strange calm came over me. I didn't even need Devon to help. These men were going down.

"Just a second. I need to get the necklace." I reached into the bag. Once my fingers were around the knife, I said a quick prayer, aimed, and, with every inch of strength and momentum, threw it. It struck the first man just above the triceps. He screamed and dropped his gun. Without wasting a second, I flung the flashlight across the room, hitting the second man between the eyes. He slumped to the floor with a loud thud. The first man pulled the knife out and went for his gun. Devon tackled him, and they struggled on the floor. I grabbed the assault weapon from the unconscious man and located the bolt handle and ammunition.

I raised the gun, aimed, and yelled, "Stop."

The man had his arm around Devon's neck and held the gun to his head.

*Shoot me, then him. It's the only way to save yourself.*

Devon's thought. His eyes locked on mine, hard and resolute.

"It's time to give up, little girl. You don't know who you're dealing with." The first man's soulless eyes narrowed.

Oh, is that right?

My vision aimed and zoomed to his right forefinger. I breathed out and fired. His finger disappeared into shards of flesh and bone, his gun dropping to the ground.

"Don't pick it up," I warned.

Devon inched toward the gun, but the first man tried to retrieve it with his good hand.

I cleared the rifle and shot both shoulders in quick succession. He rolled on the ground and shrieked.

The larger man groaned. I turned the gun his way. He lifted his head up, noticed the AK47 aimed at him, and dropped back to the floor, closing his eyes. Either he fainted or pretended to, but, in either case, it was a good move for him.

Devon grabbed my arm. "Move. Now. They have men placed in the alley. We'll need to go out the front door."

"Okay. I'll follow you."

He examined me for an extra beat.

"I've learned my lesson. I shouldn't have come. Let's go."

"I'm parked around the corner. You'll need to leave the gun."

I clutched the AK47 to my chest. "We might need it."

"The police still make unscheduled rounds, checking on the house."

I groaned. "I might regret this." I released the magazine, put the ammunition in my bag, and tucked the rifle under some bushes by the front porch.

"This way." He motioned. "I cut a hole in the fence over there. Try not to be obvious."

"We're crawling through a fence. If someone's looking, I don't think we'll fool them."

"I meant—Oh, never mind. Just be quick," he groaned.

We slipped through and strolled along the sidewalk like we didn't have a care in the world. I would have laughed if the situation weren't so serious.

Once we got into the Jeep, Devon started the engine, gunned the gas, and roared out.

"I thought we were attempting to appear calm and collected. You're driving like a maniac." I clung to the seat and door handle.

"The Jacks in the backyard were ready to go. Once they figure out we've escaped, they'll be on the road, searching for us. We don't need another shoot-out, especially since we don't have any guns." He glanced at me. "You didn't sneak any guns out, did you?

"Just the small one from . . . what were their names anyway?"

"The first one's name is John. Last time I met him, he was in a different form. I knew him as soon as he called you Sweetcakes. That man is scum."

"I took John's gun."

He rubbed his face. "We have to talk."

"I know."

"I don't want to take you back to Samara." His eyes refused to look at me.

My heart sank, and feelings of shame spread through me. "I know. I don't blame you. It was a stupid, emotional move. I put you and all the Readers at risk. I thought I could do this on my own. I'm so sorry."

My escape, my impulsive plan and what I'd done, came crashing down on me. I placed my hands over my face and cried softly. For my parents, my lost memory, and for losing my new life at Samara. "I don't deserve to go back. I'm too stupid. Or selfish. Take your pick."

"That's not the reason. I don't want you to go back unless you want to stay with me. I . . . I mean, we can't worry about you doing this again. We can't protect you on the outside."

"Okay. I understand." I wiped my nose. "It was strange how he said my memory wouldn't come back for a year. That seems like a specific guess."

"We just received a report the Jacks have a formula to simulate amnesia. Our source told us they haven't perfected it yet, so the effects wear off after about fourteen months. It's part of their strategy to inhabit new bodies. I wish we would have known this when you first came to us. Maybe we could have started on an antidote."

"You might be able to bring back my memories?"

"No promises, but there's a chance."

"Devon?"

"Yes."

"I want to go back, but only if you answer all my questions—all of them. I'm stronger now. I can handle it."

His lips curved up. "You're amazing, you know that?"

Compliments were always great, but from Devon, it was momentous.

"Why?" I asked.

"I've never seen anyone with reflexes like you. It was like

you had your plan down to within centimeters. Your aim is phenomenal."

"I want to go home."

His hands tightened on the steering wheel. "Which home?"

"Our home. Samara." A thought occurred to me. "Is Archer all right? You two are always together."

He swallowed. "I came out here without permission. It wasn't sanctioned."

"What does that mean?"

"It was considered a suicide mission. I was ordered to stay at the compound."

"You risked your life and broke a rule, for me?" My heart skipped a beat or two.

"Yeah, a few of them." His half-smile was back.

"Sorry."

"The only way I'll bring you back to Samara will be if you assure me you want to go."

"I do. I love it there. But I can't live with the secrets anymore. I want to know everything."

"All right."

"*Before* I go back into Samara."

"Okay."

"Now."

"We'll go to a safe place, and I'll tell all. I've already broken almost every rule. I might as well go for the gold."

Thank goodness. Some answers.

We drove the next half hour in silence. A crease ran between his brows and he appeared deep in thought. His driving was erratic.

"Do you have a system for losing Jacks?" I asked.

Another smirk. "Yeah. My maniac driving does the trick. We've outsmarted them so far without much problem. They try to choose the most intelligent bodies to hijack, but sometimes they aren't available." He took a sharp right onto a side street. "Don't get me wrong, Jacks can be quite devious and smart, but when they invade another human, it can decrease their mental functions by fifty percent. We think when they remove the human soul, it drains them." He shook his head. "I'm surprised they only had three or four waiting for you." He seemed to think about it for a moment. "But I'm sure they didn't expect Rambo."

I vaguely remembered watching the movie with Archer last month. "Wasn't Rambo a man?" That was insulting.

"Yes, but you fight better than any man I've seen. You had those two Jacks down in about five seconds. Impressive." This time he met my eyes and smiled. The adrenaline from the fight had disappeared, and I looked at him. Really looked. Handsome, strong . . . and he risked everything to save me. Gratitude and something else, maybe affection, swirled inside my chest.

*Shut it down.*

With a deep breath and a change of subject, I asked, "Will everyone be angry with me? Can you tell them I'm sorry, and I wouldn't have gone if I'd known the risk to them?"

"They know. The first year is the hardest for the new Readers. The last couple hundred years have turned up only five. We think you're the last one. That's why everyone is after you. The Readers want to keep you safe. Whereas the Jacks just want to use you as their pawn to protect them when the big war begins."

"How would I protect them?"

"Just being in their custody. They know we wouldn't attack another Reader. Too risky. Especially since you might be the Lost One."

"Do you think I am? You know, the Lost One? It seems I'd instinctively know something that big."

"You wouldn't, especially if the Jacks gave you a memory wipe. In time, all your normal functions should return."

That was good news. At least there would be a chance my memories—my family, my life—would someday come back.

He pulled the car onto a dirt road. "Okay, we're close to the river. We'll be exposed to possible drones for these last few miles. You'll need to get in back and stay hidden. The toolbox should do the trick."

"Ha. Yeah, right." There was no way; I would barely fit in that toolbox.

"The Jacks will be everywhere. They'll be desperate now they believe we might have the Lost One. I tried to convince them you weren't, but I'm sure they saw through it." He started to get out of the car. "Once we get to the river, the trees will shield us. In the meantime . . ."

I remained in my seat and leaned forward, taking big gulps of air. Tingles spread throughout my body, but, this time, it wasn't from Devon's touch—it was from a lack of oxygen.

"What's going on?" His voice had an edge.

"Claus . . . claustro . . . phobia."

"I thought you were over that. You escaped out a tube, for God's sake. How did you manage that?"

"With . . . with a big, fat rat, too." I laughed through my labored breathing. "I wanted to find out what happened . . ." I tried to get my breathing to even out. "To my parents. I also . . . also wanted to see if I could get my memories back." I fisted my hands. "I hate it . . . not knowing anything about myself. It feels like I'm isolated from the world, oblivious to the difference between reality and lies."

Devon squatted next to the open car door. "I'm sorry, but we don't have time for this. I promise to tell you everything when we get to the river. No more waiting."

The promise of information motivated me. He was right, if I could squeeze through a tube, knowing I could get stuck, I could handle a large box. I got out of the car and walked to the back. He opened the lid, and I examined the space. A little bigger than the tube, that was good.

"How long will I be in there?" I asked.

"Ten minutes at the most. I'll leave the top ajar." He removed a few items to make room for me.

"Make it fast." I jumped in and curled up into the small space, closing my eyes. Why couldn't the Jacks have wiped out this part of my memory?

After bumping and bouncing over uneven dirt roads, the Jeep came to a stop.

"You still alive back there?" Devon shouted.

I contemplated hitting him with my flashlight again.

"Haha. Now get me out, right now!"

He opened the lid, and I hopped out. I bent over and took in large lungfuls of fresh air. After a few minutes, I was ready to go. The rushing sound of the river nearby beckoned me.

"Come on. We'll go down the river and you can grill me." He walked past and headed toward a large storage shed. After tugging open the door, he pulled out a fully inflated raft, dragging it toward the shore.

"You're not serious," I said.

He stopped and cocked his head. "You don't have a fear of water, do you?"

"Well, uh, no. But why can't we, you know, just drive through the gatehouse like before?"

"We use this back way whenever we feel there might be a threat of exposure. The Jacks know we're in the area and will have every single one of them on the lookout on any of the main roads." He handed me a paddle. "Let's go."

# CHAPTER 16

Devon stowed the Jeep in the large storage shed, and we walked back to the shore. "Here, get in so you don't get your feet wet, and I'll drag the raft in." He'd taken off his shoes and rolled up his pants.

"It won't rip the bottom? I don't want to put any holes in it before we get started." I leaned forward to get a good look down the river. I wouldn't consider it raging, but it was deep and swift.

"It's reinforced. These rafts have a self-bailing system." He waved his hand toward the boat. "Get in."

"How long will this take?" I stepped into the raft and sat on the bench.

"About a half-hour. So, have those questions ready. Once we get to the compound, I'll be back to my usual."

"Mute?"

He hopped in the boat, smiled, and grabbed the oars.

"Let's start with my parents."

"Sure. That's a good place to start." He maneuvered the raft into the center of the river. "We found out about your family six months ago. Your parents worked as professors at North Seattle University."

The wind hit my face, making my hair fly in every direction. "Yeah, yeah. I know." I twirled my finger in the air, giving him the hurry up signal.

The river slowed to a crawl. Devon pushed the oars forward and leaned back.

"How did you first hear about us?" I asked.

"We believe your parents reached out to us through an article they wrote about mind-reading. We thought it was a call for help, but didn't know for sure."

We went around a slight bend, and the river started to pick up. Devon grabbed tight to the oars and said, "Hang onto the rope handles on each side."

I closed my eyes and held on. After we passed through a section with white water rapids and large rocks, I let my death grip relax. Once the river smoothed out again, I started back with my questions.

"Back to my parents. I read articles on them at the library. I know about their lives, but can you tell me what they were like?" I held my breath and waited.

He grinned. "They were funny. A little like you."

I probably looked funny with my wet hair sticking out in every direction.

"Did they seem nice? Were they happy?"

"Yes and yes." He navigated around a large boulder.

Those were the two most important questions about my parents. Now that I knew, I could settle back and enjoy the view.

"What was their favorite dinner?"

He shook his head. "Spaghetti and meatballs. Your mom made it three times a week."

"Sports?"

"Seahawks."

"Movies?"

"*Pride and Prejudice.* I think you and your mom watched it once a week." He smiled.

A mental note to self: reserve the movie at the Hub when we returned. "Okay, moving on. How about hobbies?

"Reading."

Warmth swirled through my chest, giving me a glowing, happy feeling. It was nice to know I remembered something basic to tie me to my parents.

"Why don't Readers have children?"

His face froze, and he stopped rowing. "That was a jump of subject I wasn't expecting."

"I'm sorry, but I have so many questions, and I can't seem to organize them. Is that okay?"

He laughed and looked to the sky. "This is going to be a long night, isn't it?"

"Yes. Very long. Back to the children. What's up with that?"

"We're not sure. All we know is, the Readers will be able to have children again once things are resolved after the war. As you know, the Seers couldn't predict the winner. But they did say the winning side would be able to bring more children into the world."

"So, no children on either side until after the war?"

"Yes."

"Do you want the war?"

"Yes and no." His eyes swept down the river. "To be honest, after all these years, I have doubts it will ever happen."

"Yeah. I can see why. It's been a long time." I paused. "Why can I hear you? I mean, some of your thoughts."

"That's a tough one. The Elders think it might have something to do with your amnesia, that your reading ability is heightened because your brain is clear."

"That makes sense. But why just you? I haven't heard anyone else."

"They believe you're picking up on my emotions. I tend to get a little wound up sometimes." He shrugged.

I laughed. "If that's the case, I should be hearing Lucy loud and clear."

"You're right. You'll probably pick up on her thoughts next."

Lucy and I spent almost every waking moment together. Wouldn't a thought or two have slipped by already?

"Do you need any help with the rowing? I could take over so you can rest."

"I've got it. If we see any drones, we'll need to pull out to the side."

"How about money? How do you finance all this?"

A smile and a mischievous gleam in his eyes told me their source of funding might be unorthodox.

"Las Vegas." Another smile and shrug. "We take shifts."

No need to explain more.

I tilted my head skyward. The trees on each side of the river stretched out, almost touching. "I can see why you'd take this path to the compound. With the trees shielding us, it would be hard for even a drone to pick us up."

"That's the idea," he said with a nod.

"Do you like the river?" I wasted a little time asking this question, but I didn't care.

"Love it."

Back to business. "Do you know how many Jacks there are?"

"We believe there are over five thousand. They're a sneaky bunch, so it's hard to pinpoint an exact number."

"Wow. You're really outnumbered."

"You mean *we're* outnumbered." He smirked.

"Yeah." I laughed. "Thanks for reminding me."

"Anytime." He reclined back and let the boat coast.

"Lucy told me that a Jack can't take control of a Reader. Is that true?"

"Yes. They've tried, believe me. We have natural powers making it impossible for them to gain control."

My shoulders relaxed a little. "That's good." I pondered my next question for a moment. "Lucy mentioned the Jacks had a campaign against humanity. What's that all about?"

"It's complicated, but I'll try to explain. Every Jack's survival depends on them taking over another adult human body. It has to be done without family or friends noticing. The key is for them to remain undiscovered. In the beginning, their main focus was to create situations that would convince tribe or world leaders to start wars. It would separate families and give them the opportunity to take control. At the end of a war, the Jack would move in and live the life of their human. The change in personality could be attributed to the trauma of war."

"So the Jacks would create wars just to separate family and friends?"

"Yes. As the world became larger, and with the creation of nuclear weapons, it's been more difficult for them to convince world leaders to wage war."

"What did they do instead?"

"For one, they helped with the creation of the Internet."

"Why would the Internet be helpful to the Jacks? It brings people together, not apart."

"From outside appearances, yes, more people connect and interact. In truth, the ability to stay at home to interact, isolates people. Think about it. How many Facebook, Twitter, or Instagram friends get together in person on a regular basis? Or better yet, come hold your hand when a friend or family member dies? I'll answer that—not many. In times of crisis, a person might get a thumbs up or receive a few words of support, but they don't know each other on a deeper level. People, a lot of times, don't know their friends' quirks or preferences. Or, in some cases, not even their personality traits. The social networks have created what we call social isolation. It's disconnection at its worst."

"So the Jacks have an easier time taking over their bodies without detection with so many people lulled into the façade of connection." Diabolical, that's what they were.

"Yes." He guided the raft around another slight bend in the river.

"Why cause so much death and chaos if there are only five thousand of them?"

"For them, it's a game. They thrive on the power and control. Also, they're quite picky. After a war or conflict, they have a huge pool to choose from."

"What else are they doing?"

"Drugs, alcohol—you name it. Everything negative associated with the human race has come from the Jacks. None of us were meant for hatred, greed, murder—"

"They have to be stopped." I clenched my hands. A resolve to help filled me with determination.

He ran his fingers through his messy, black hair. "I know."

"You seem hesitant."

"I love my life. I love—"

"Yes?"

"Everything. When we go to war, we'll risk it all." He glanced toward the shoreline.

"Tell me about the other compound in Colorado." With hands on knees, I bent closer.

He took a deep breath, held it for a moment, then let it out. "It's not a good place."

Not what I expected to hear. "What do you mean?"

"It's a prison. We have seventeen Readers who've committed the worst possible crime."

"Murder?"

"Yes. All of them. They'll never be released." He shook his head and frowned. A crease formed between his brows.

"For eternity?" I shivered. "I can't even imagine."

"We can't risk it. Even if they were rehabilitated, the potential is there for them to take another life." He took a deep inhale.

"What's it like? Have you ever been there?"

The boat bounced off a large rock, and I grabbed hold of the handles again.

"About fifty years ago. It's bad. The cells are small and dark. Their freedom is gone in every sense of the word." He reached down and picked up the oars. "Most of them have lost their minds. I can't blame them."

"What type of people were they? I mean, what would possess them to risk losing eternity?"

"We have the benefit of time—learning and knowledge. But for some of the Readers, emotions can still override good judgment. In every single case, it was a crime of passion."

"Like a love triangle?"

"Yes. It's the common thread with every prisoner."

"I have another question, but this one you don't have to answer."

He dipped the oars into the water and began rowing. I smiled to myself, imagining he wanted to get to the compound faster, to get away from all my questions.

He paused and tilted his head. "I want to know about *your* parents." I chewed on my lip and waited.

"They died protecting the Seers." He stopped rowing. "My mom, she was brave, like you. You would've liked her."

"You think I'm brave?" Warmth radiated through my chest. "Not in the category of reckless?"

"That too." He smiled and, darn, that dimple on his right cheek appeared and did all sorts of fluttery things to my stomach. He leaned forward. "And kind of infuriating."

"Who, me?"

"Yeah." He tucked a strand of loose hair behind my ear. "I like your haircut. It's not too short."

With my heart about to beat out of my chest, I asked, "How about the color?"

"It's good. Beauti—" He stopped "We're almost there."

"Wait. I have more questions."

He eyed me. "One, maybe two."

"What's your favorite color?" Would he answer? I wanted to get at least one piece of information that was personal just to him.

He continued to stare, his gaze shifting to each of my eyes. "Blue."

"Dark or light?"

"After the sun sets, there's a bright, vibrant blue that's right above the other shades. It's rare, stunning. When I see that color, it's hard for me to look away."

We sat a few feet apart, his eyes locked on mine. He moved toward me, but snapped back and grabbed the oars. "The others are waiting for us. I don't want them to worry."

"My last question." With my heart thumping erratically, I asked what I really needed to know. "Do you feel anything unusual when we touch?" There, I asked. No going back.

His eyes darted away, and he cleared his throat. "Uh, no. Nothing out of the ordinary."

Confirmation. I was a Devon Groupie. How embarrassing.

"Just checking." Blood rushed to my face, and tears filled my eyes. Please, God, don't let them escape.

"Even if I were to feel anything . . . unusual, it wouldn't be a good idea to explore it, not right now anyway."

Blinking, I asked, "What do you mean?"

"As soon as the Soul Mates connect, the war will be

immediate." He shook his head. "We're not ready."

My eyes blinked one too many times. A big, fat tear rolled down my cheek.

He swiped it with his thumb and drew back, wincing before he put his hand under his armpit and bent over.

"What's the matter? Are you okay?"

His eyes squeezed shut. He stuttered out, "Yes . . . yes, give me a second. I have a cramp in my hand." He straightened and shook his hand out, still in obvious pain.

"Are we close to the compound? Doc has ice packs you can put on it."

"Yes, we're here." He stood up and leaned over, making the raft list. Startled by the motion, I stumbled on the rope and went right over the side.

# CHAPTER 17

FREEZING COLD WATER HIT me, like glaciers-in-Alaska freezing. Or, that would be my best guess since I was pretty certain I'd never been dropped into a glacier or river before. Oh, the burning. I surfaced and drew in a huge gulp of air, but I couldn't move the rest of my body. Devon jumped from the raft, grabbed me by the arm, and dragged me to the shore.

"Ann, I'm so sorry. I've never done . . . I mean, I can't believe that happened. Come with me. I have a blanket in the Jeep."

My legs were still stiff, but I was able to follow him up the path. With my body shivering, he guided me to another large shed tucked back into the woods. He unlocked the door, searched the back seat of the Jeep, retrieved a wool blanket, and tossed it to me. "That should do the trick."

"Did you do . . . did you tip the raft?" I held up a finger, trying to stop my teeth from chattering. "On purpose?"

"No. Of course not. It just shifted a little. I just, I mean, I didn't think you'd go over."

He's lying.

He felt *me and* my pain. But he'd rather dump me in the water than answer my questions. Why? Was it really the war he worried about, or was I—what did he call me? Infuriating. That's right. I got into another Jeep and slammed the door shut. Fine. If he wanted distance, he'd get it.

"Ann?"

I turned away and didn't answer.

"Uh. If you give me the door handle, I can attach it later," he said.

I looked down, and, sure enough, clutched in my right hand was the chrome handle. My eyes widened. "I'm so sorry."

He smiled. "The Jeep is old. I'm sure it was loose."

*Quit being nice. You're making it worse.*

I placed the handle on the console between us and rubbed my hands in front of the heater. When we approached another guardhouse on the back of the property, my stomach dropped. "Oh, no. I didn't get the guard in trouble for slipping past him, did I?"

"No, not at all. Samara, unlike the complex in Colorado, isn't a prison. Readers are free to leave anytime. He's only stationed there to give us a heads-up in case the Jacks try to breach the entrance."

"Why haven't I been given access to leave then? I haven't been included in the drills either."

"Because of your amnesia. The Elders feared you might become emotional and take off—putting your life, and ours, at risk." He glanced at me.

"Got it." I rubbed my forehead.

"Don't worry about it. No one is angry. Just concerned."

Devon entered the compound and parked the Jeep. Before I could figure out what to do with the door, Lucy opened it and flung herself at me, squealing, "You're safe. You're safe."

I patted her back. "You're strangling me."

"Oh." She pulled me from the Jeep to continue the hug. "It's all my fault. I should have told you everything. All of our girl talks, and I kept things from you. If anything had happened . . ." She squeezed me tighter, her head on my shoulder. Tears—or was that snot?—leaked onto my shirt.

"No, it's my mistake. I'm so sorry I worried you."

She clung to me. "Okay. But I'm telling you everything now. I don't care what the Elders say or think." Her eyes pleaded with Devon. "Don't tell."

"I've already told her all, so you don't have to worry about any more slips."

Her mouth fell open. "Wow. Everything?"

He nodded.

"Oh, the Elders want you at a meeting in an hour."

"Great." He groaned. "That should be fun."

"You're wet." She looked back and forth between us. "Why are you both wet?"

"We came down the river and had a little mishap." I glanced at Devon, and he gave a little shrug.

"Let's get you inside and warm." Lucy turned back to me, touching my shoulder-length hair. "It's so pretty. I love the dark color. Now, I want to hear all the details. Tell me everything."

"Well, I stabbed and shot a man, another was hit in the head with a flashlight. I stole a car, well, a couple different cars. I robbed a store—"

"Oh, stop! You're so funny. Let's get some pizza, and you can tell me what really happened."

I shrugged. "Okay." I let her take my hand and lead me away from Devon.

Two weeks later, and Devon still avoided me, making sure there were a good five feet between us at all times.

Susie was a different story, though. She had her hands all over Devon and Archer. She'd embrace them to say hello, to say goodbye, when she was excited—any reason seemed to elicit affection from her. It didn't have to be much either. Sushi for dinner warranted a round of hugs.

For the most part, Susie kept her distance from me. She adopted a sympathetic air when I arrived back at Samara and was, oh, so sorry, about the newscast debacle at her birthday party. With wide eyes and hand over her heart, she proclaimed a false innocence, claiming to have no idea who could have done such a terrible thing. Of course, Archer and Devon were in attendance and ate it up. They assured her they'd find the culprit. I wanted to tell them the perpetrator stood right before them, but I didn't have the evidence to prove my suspicions.

"Come on." Devon motioned with his head.

"Who, me?" Alone in the Hub for a little quiet time before my next class, I was momentarily confused.

"Anyone else sitting at your table?" A half-smirk and a raised eyebrow followed his question.

I stuffed my books into my bag. Wait. I didn't want to appear desperate for his company or anything. "I *am* rather busy."

"I can tell. Just get your things, and let's get going." He took a few steps away and turned back. I hadn't moved yet. Crossed arms, a tapping foot, and an exasperated sigh followed.

Ugh. "All right. What's so important anyway?"

"You liked the waterfalls, right?"

"I loved the waterfalls. Are we going there?" *Say yes.*

"No."

"Do I have to guess, or are you going to tell me?" Patience was not one of my virtues.

"You won't be able to guess. Hurry up or we'll miss it."

With my bag slung over my shoulder, I followed him out of the Hub. He walked at a quick pace, and I found myself run/walking to keep up with him. "Do you want me to come, or are you trying to ditch me?" I laughed.

He tapped his watch. "We only have a few minutes." His long legs slowed a little. After a few more turns, he said, "We're here."

"Oh, I know where we are. This is the hot house and rainforest chamber. Lucy promised me a tour next week."

"Your tour has come early. We keep it locked, most of the time, careful to keep the temperature steady." He put his hand against the pad. "I have a reservation. We'll slip in quickly."

The door clicked open, and he motioned me in.

I followed and stopped just inside the door. Gorgeous. Vibrant reds, yellows, purples, and greens burst from the dense foliage and lush plants that filled the space from floor to ceiling. The sweet scent of orchids—heavenly.

"Hey, who painted that?" I pointed to a mural on the back wall. A dozen different flower species, plants, and wildlife covered the entire surface. The beauty of it was more like an extension of the environment than a painting.

"Oh, that. I did. Come on."

"Get out. You're an artist?"

"I paint a little."

"A little?" Impressed, I stared a little longer. "It's so realistic. I feel like I'm in a different world."

"There's more. Follow me."

We weaved past huge leaves partially blocking the small path leading to the back of the room.

"Wow. It's hot and humid in here." I fanned my face. A little better, but my skin was already coated with moisture.

"We keep it at eighty degrees with ninety percent humidity."

"That explains why I'm drenched already." I laughed and pulled my t-shirt away from my body in an effort to cool myself off. Devon's hair had started to curl, and tiny water droplets formed on his lashes.

*Nice.*

His fingers combed through his hair. "Where was I? Oh, right." He cleared his throat. "There's something I don't think you've experienced yet. I usually come alone, but I thought you might like to get in on the action."

Action? I took a step back, worried about a rainforest creature making an appearance. "Are there animals in here?"

He shook his head. "Not that kind of action. A storm."

My rapid heartbeat slowed a little. "No jaguars or sloths ready to attack?"

"No, you can relax."

"What do you mean when you say storm?"

"It's a simulated storm. Do you like rain and wind?"

Hmm. "I hadn't considered it. I'd guess, living in Seattle for so long, I either love or hate them."

"You're about to find out. We collect rain and snow from the top of Samara and fill huge vats with the run-off. We take turns recycling some of it for a simulated storm inside the glass partition over there. It feels great; you'll love it." He pointed to a walled off area. "I get five minutes a month and I'm giving it to you."

"Why?"

He paused and rubbed the stubble on his chin. "I've never really had a chance to say I'm sorry."

"For being a jerk?" *Oops.* "I mean, for being . . . difficult?"

That rare smile of his made an appearance. So bright, it about knocked the wind out of me. I thought about looking away, but my eyes stayed locked on his instead. His smile slipped, and he stepped closer.

"Not for that," he said in a low voice.

"Oh?" That's all my brain could muster. With him close, my thoughts scattered.

"I wanted to tell you how sorry I am for everything that's happened to you. Losing your parents, having your memory wiped, and being hunted by the Jacks. I know it can't be easy."

*Whoa.* He understood. My feelings of loss and sadness started to surface, but other feelings—warmth and gratitude— took over. My throat constricted, and I was able to say, "Thanks."

He smiled again, and I considered taking the extra step and wrapping myself around him. How would he react? Before I could find out, he stepped back and asked, "Are you ready?"

"Yes!" But then I realized he was only referring to the storm. I'd need some rain and wind to douse my overactive imagination.

"Great." He pulled open a panel and pushed buttons. "A downpour with wind?" he asked.

"Where does the wind come from?" I asked.

He punched another button and two large doors opened mid-height on separate walls. Huge fans sat behind the panels. "All these plants produce an excess of oxygen. We use the fans to push the air into those vents." He pointed to six large openings in the ceiling. "From there, it's circulated throughout the compound."

"Cool."

"Let's get started."

I glanced down at my outfit. Oh well, I guess a little more water wouldn't hurt.

He opened a closet and tossed me a raincoat.

He was always a step ahead. I laughed and asked, "You sure you can't read my mind?"

"I wish," he said under his breath. "You're just easy to read. Not mind-read, but every expression that passes over your face is an open door to your thoughts."

That wasn't good. I'd have to work on that. "Is that why you always win at poker night?"

"Yep. You in for the storm?" A devilish grin spread across his face.

"Okay." I tried to act nonchalant, but I wanted to jump up and down with excitement.

"Do you want a light rain shower or a full-fledged storm?"

"Oh!" I gave a hop. So much for reining it in.

"That's what I thought. Storm?" He smirked.

"Not a hurricane or anything. How about twenty miles per hour? That's pretty windy isn't it?"

"Sure, thirty miles per hour it is." He chuckled. "Grab the raincoat, stand in the middle, and I'll close the doors."

"Are you sure you want to give up your turn?"

"I'm sure."

My stomach dipped.

*Don't read too much into it.*

I put on the raincoat and stood in the middle of the enclosed area. The click of the glass doors closing meant it would start soon. Devon had his back to me as he punched buttons inside the wall panel. A small amount of rain began to fall, splattering on the foliage and the top of my hood, the sound soothing. I took a deep, cleansing breath and enjoyed the sensation. I turned to Devon and mouthed "more" and he nodded. Almost at once, the rain went from a pitter patter to a downpour. Closing my eyes, I tilted my head to the ceiling and let the large water droplets plop onto my face, cooling me, but also setting loose a torrent of emotions. The stress of the past couple months seemed to melt away, like the water from my skin. I slipped off the raincoat and tossed it on a nearby bush, wanting to soak in every drop. I'd never felt so alive. I stretched out my arms and laughed. The wind picked up, and my wet hair whipped against my face. Exhilaration and happiness flooded through me.

I'd almost forgotten about Devon until I heard, *Damn, this is torture.*

I turned to face him. He stood on the other side of the glass with his head tilted wearing a strange expression.

I mouthed, "What?"

The rain and wind immediately stopped. Five minutes had

gone fast. Devon walked back into the room with a towel and said, "I guess that clears up the mystery of whether you like wind or rain."

I shook off his confusing thought and odd expression. "I loved it. When can I do it again?"

# CHAPTER 18

"DID YOU HEAR THE news?" Lucy's eyebrows wagged up and down. She sat next to me at our usual table at the Hub. Devon and Archer perked up.

"What news?"

"Markus is coming back tomorrow." She giggled.

Devon gave her a double-take. "Are you sure? I heard he'd be gone until next week."

"The rumor mill says he's excited to get back to meet someone." She grinned at me.

"What the—He can't come waltzing back here, acting like he's the prince." Archer's scowl matched Devon's glower.

"They're jealous," Lucy whispered in my ear.

Well, good.

"Come on, Devon. We have to help Doc with surgery." Archer pulled his arm. Devon hesitated, but got up from his chair. He narrowed his eyes at Lucy, while Archer coaxed him out the door.

"Things always liven up when Markus gets back from one of his trips. He has lots of energy." Lucy smiled and winked.

"What do you mean by energy?"

She lowered her voice. "He loves women. I mean, *really* loves them."

Ahh. "He's a player?"

"Big time."

"Why didn't you mention this before? I don't know, maybe a warning or something."

"For you? No, you'd never fall for someone like him. He has a harem of around twenty that follow him around."

"Archer and Devon also have women making excuses to get near them. Of course, Susie is the worst, but we can't go anywhere without fifty sets of eyes on us."

"Archer and Devon don't *entertain* them like Markus does."

"Oh." That wasn't good.

"Yeah. The Elders have talked to Markus about it. I think even Devon's had words with him. But he hasn't changed. To be honest, I don't think the women care about his habits. They want to spend time with him, however brief."

I chuckled. "You can leave me off that list."

"It's different with the new Readers, though."

"How so?"

"A few of them were so desperate to be his match, they were like—you know the children's story of Cinderella?"

"Yes. I have it in my bookshelf. The one with the evil stepmother?"

She laughed. "Yes, but the new Readers were more like the stepsisters trying to wedge their foot into the glass slipper. I wouldn't have been surprised if they applied electrodes to him to spark a connection."

I giggled. "That bad?"

"Yes. After the obligatory kiss, the women would fawn all over him, professing their connection and undying love. He'd just shrug and say, 'Nope. Don't feel anything.' There've been many tears."

"He sounds like a jerk."

"But that's the problem. He isn't. He's quite charming and funny." She paused and looked off into the distance. "He's also one of my best friends."

"Would you, you know, *like* him, if he were more— singular?" I asked.

She perched her head onto her linked hands. "I can't even entertain the possibility. You know, with each of us named as the possible Soul Mate to the Lost One. I think that might be the reason Markus hops around from each relationship. One can get lonely."

"Yeah, I can see how it would." I grabbed her hand.

"I'm okay. I've adjusted. Hey, maybe you'll end up being the Lost One with Markus as your Soul Mate." She grinned. "If that's the case, you'll need to straighten him out."

"It sounds like a major overhaul." I laughed.

"It would be nice, though. Even if it signaled the war, at least there'd be resolution." Her eyes met mine. "I'd hoped it was you and Devon, probably because I already feel like you're my sister."

"Aw. I feel the same way. Aren't you worried about the war though?"

"Yeah. Devon doesn't think we're ready yet. But the Elders have come up with a few possible strategies that might just work. So, while I'm worried, I'm still confident." She squeezed my hand. "Can you imagine? Human beings could go back to their natural instincts for love and creativity. Without the Jacks, harmony would be restored."

"What about the Readers who've committed murder?"

"In three thousand years, there've been seventeen, all occurring after the Seers died."

"Oh. That is a low percentage."

"I also think a lot had to do with our confinement. We get out when we need to, but sometimes people forget and become a little antsy. It's happened to me on occasion. Once the Jacks are gone, we can go back to living in complete freedom."

"Aren't some Readers disturbed living on the outside? I know I didn't like reading thoughts. That woman in the store called me a bimbo!" I said, fisting my hands in anger.

"You're still angry about that?" She laughed and patted my arm. "We're still evolving and learning new skills. We're trying to learn how to switch our ability on and off when needed. For instance, we try to keep our minds quiet and not read unless we want to eavesdrop. I can do it about half the time."

"After the war, would you want to live outside Samara?"

"Yes, I think all of us would. I love it here, but I hope this place can be more for reunions or weddings. I enjoy meeting new people and making friends. A life without the Jacks would make that possible." She put her hand on her heart. "Everything would be possible."

People gathered at the entry, and an excited buzz went through the room. "What's going on?" I asked Lucy.

"I don't know." She stood on her tiptoes and tried to look over the heads gathered by the entry.

I stood, but couldn't see. The crowd parted a little, and Devon, Archer and, holy wow, another man was with them.

"Who is *that?*" I asked.

"Markus is early." She smiled and waved at him, trying to get his attention while his fan club surrounded him.

"You didn't tell me he was so . . . so . . ."

"Gorgeous? Handsome?" She laughed. "What did you expect?"

I didn't expect to be drawn to him like I was. It wasn't just his looks. He exuded something I couldn't put my finger on. But it made me want to get close to him to figure out what it was. No, it made me want to get away. Ugh. Already one groupie, I didn't want to add another to my list. I eyed the doorway, planning a quick exit.

About to make my move, my eyes glanced back and locked on Markus. Wavy, brown hair, electric-blue eyes, high cheekbones, rugged jaw, and a playful smile. I tried to look away, but couldn't.

He put his hand on his chest and mouthed the word 'Wow' in my direction. I tore my eyes away to look behind me. Nope. No one there.

He walked toward me at a quick pace, brushing past the hands trying to hold him back. I eyed my exit again and took a calming breath. Nope. Didn't work. My heart pounded, and I thought I was shaking, but I couldn't feel my body, so I wasn't sure.

"Uh oh," Lucy whispered.

"What? What?" My voice came out raspy.

Markus stopped directly in front of me and said, "I think I'm in love."

My mind froze. Before I could respond, Markus put his arm around my waist, pulled me close, and pressed his lips to mine. Oh, how he kissed me. I closed my eyes for a second, enjoying the sensation.

I pulled back. Wait. What was I doing?

He groaned and pulled me closer. "I take it back. I know I'm in love. Did you feel that?" he asked. His lips were about to make contact again, but a large hand ripped him away. Devon. He reared back and punched Markus in the face, knocking him to the floor.

*Get your playboy hands off her. She's mine.*

Markus yelled, "Don't interfere with this, Devon. She's the one. I felt it this time. Do you hear me? She's the Lost One, and I'm her Soul Mate. Back off."

# CHAPTER 19

Lucy YANKED MY ARM. "Let's get out of here before it gets ugly."

"Before?"

"Okay. Uglier. Move it." She pulled harder.

"Ouch. Quit tugging at me. I'll go. But shouldn't we make sure they've quit fighting first?" A large group surrounded Markus and Devon. Angry words were still being tossed around, but the voices in the crowd made it impossible to hear them clearly.

"You being here guarantees the fight will continue. The best thing we can do is leave. Come on."

We made it out into the quiet corridor, and it hit me. I heard Devon. I couldn't hide my smile.

"I'd be smiling, too. Markus. I can't believe it!" Lucy wound her arms around my neck in a tight hug.

"No, no. That's not why I'm smiling. You're strangling me again." I attempted to unwrap her death grip.

"Strangling, oh, sorry." She moved back a little and tilted her head. "Why the smile?"

"Because. Well, because Devon got so . . . protective."

Her face went blank. "Oh. Devon. He must have had feelings for you all along. He has to be so . . ." Her chin trembled. "You'll let him down easy, won't you?"

"Yes. I mean, no." What to say? "I'm confused right now. Can we talk about this later?"

"Sure. I'm happy for you, really." She waved her hand in front of her face while blinking back tears. "Devon will be fine." She lost the battle and burst out crying.

"Aw, Lucy. It's going to be okay, I promise. Everything will work out as it should." I rubbed her back. I didn't want to spill everything until I had things figured out.

"Sorry for getting all teary-eyed. I'm probably making you feel horrible." She took the sleeve of her shirt and wiped her nose. It reminded me of something a five-year-old would do, and I laughed.

"Come on. Let's get you some tissues."

Lucy calmed down a little, and, after making sure she was tucked in her room with a big box of tissues, I headed back to my room.

I rounded the last turn and stopped. Susie stood right in front of my door, body rigid, arms crossed.

"Susie." I already suspected why she was there.

"You are one stupid girl." All pretense of niceness gone. "I warned you what would happen. Now you can live with the consequences." And with her signature flip of hair, she stomped off.

Great. What was she up to now? I had a feeling it'd be

worse than the radio broadcast.

Tea. That would help. I threw a few logs into the fireplace, fixed myself a cup of tea, and sat down on the sofa, prepared to figure everything out.

*I'm floating . . . floating above the compound. The scenery beneath me is breathtaking, with blossom-covered trees and a gentle river snaking its way through the forest. A bird flies by, a blue jay, I think. A sense of peace and love for my home fills me.*

*Something glows right in the center of the compound. A light? Orange and red, it grows larger and larger and turns to blue flames.*

*Oh, no.*

*My home bursts apart at the seams. Smoke and fire, steam and debris, shoot straight up and out. Devon's Jeep, melted, sails past me. The people I love all gone in an instant from the fiery explosion.*

I sucked in a huge breath, almost as if I'd been underwater. I sat on the couch with the same cup of tea trembling in my hand. The lights low, a fire still burning. I must have dozed off. Had that been a dream or a vision?

A shadow a few feet away startled me, making me spill the lukewarm liquid. My hands fisted in preparation for a fight.

"It's me."

"Devon?"

"Yes, sorry to wake you." He stepped into the light and took a seat next to me. "I had to come."

"I'm not sure if I was asleep, but . . . Devon, I saw something horrible. I think it might have been a vision."

"A vision?"

"It was here . . . Samara. It blew up right before my eyes. Do you think the war's about to begin?"

"It depends. That's why I'm here." He hesitated and his eyes cast down. "When the Soul Mates connect, it will signal the beginning of the war. Markus has declared you to be his match."

"Yes, I heard."

He sat next to me on the sofa. "Did you feel it? With him?" he whispered.

So much emotion came from those few words. His voice wrapped around me, wanting and hopeful.

"I felt . . . shocked. I don't know how I'm supposed to feel."

"I want to touch you," he said.

"Why now? You've been avoiding me for months. Are you doing this because you're jealous? Is it just because of Markus?"

"I'm ready to know the truth. And yes, I'm jealous. Profoundly." He scooted closer. "Can you tell me? Did you have a connection with Markus?"

"I honestly don't know. Won't it take time?"

"Let's see." He picked up my hand and intertwined our fingers.

A warmth started from my fingers and worked its way up my arm. I closed my eyes and let the sensation pulse through my body, spreading into every cell.

Euphoria. Happiness.

Love.

My soul opened up, beckoning him, and we joined almost

like our clasped hands. The warm tingles turned into sparks, firing through me, uncontrolled.

He took my face in his hands, and our eyes connected, the heat within so intense, it was almost unbearable. Out of breath, I shook my head, knowing I was on the edge. The emotions were too strong, too powerful, I couldn't contain them.

"Too much," I said.

"I know. I didn't know it would be like this . . . so intense." His eyes closed, and he rested his head against my forehead, running his hands through my hair. "Don't be afraid."

He moved back a little and looked at my lips. "Ready?"

Was I? It didn't matter because there was nothing that would stop me. I gripped his t-shirt and pulled him to me. He smiled a little and grazed his lips over mine, once, twice. My hands glided through his wavy hair, and I sighed. His light kiss turned passionate as his hands gripped me, pulling me to him. Our bodies pressed closer, as if we were trying to melt into each other. We broke apart for a moment, out of breath.

He held my shoulders. "Oh God, Ann, what have we done?"

I smoothed my hand over the stubble on his cheek. "What do you—"

Loud alarms began to ring.

"The Jacks. The war's begun."

# CHAPTER 20

T HE DOORS BURST OPEN and Archer's dad, Mr. Gallagher, entered my room, followed by three other Elders and two armed guards.

Devon jumped up from the couch. "Have the Jacks breached security?"

Mr. Gallagher connected eyes with me then turned to address Devon. "No. No signs of any Jacks yet. We have to ask you to come with us, Devon."

"Why?" I asked.

"There's been an incident we need to discuss with Devon, Miss Baker."

Why was he so formal with me? A pit formed in my stomach.

"What kind of incident?" Devon asked Archer's dad. The two security men lifted their guns and pointed them at Devon.

"Why are you pointing guns at him? What's going on?" My mouth went dry, and I began to shake.

"Yeah. I'd like to know that, as well." Devon glanced around at each man.

"Your fingerprints were on the knife, Devon." Mr. Gallagher said.

Devon's brow furrowed. "What knife? What are you talking about?"

Lucy stormed into the room. "Tell me it isn't true! Markus can't be dead!"

I gasped. "Wha . . . Markus?" No! Oh, dear God, no.

Devon's jaw dropped, and his face drained of color. "It can't be," he whispered.

Lucy stood in front of Devon and faced the men. "Put those guns down. He didn't do it, and you know it."

"We have evidence that suggests otherwise. Markus was killed with a single knife wound between the third and fourth rib, left side, killing him within moments. There are very few people who know this technique." Mr. Gallagher shook his head. "We've run the prints from the knife and they're a match with Devon." His eyes turned to Devon again, his expression conflicted. "We can't take the chance."

"Devon wouldn't do that. This is a set-up!" I yelled. "Susie was here earlier, threatening something like this. She's trying to get back at Devon for not choosing her."

Mr. Gallagher turned back to me. "It will all come out in the tribunal."

Archer burst into the room. "Dad." He looked at the men, the guns. His eyes were red and swollen. "I was with Devon the entire night. He couldn't have done it. I want to find whoever did this to Markus." He stopped and collected himself. "But it wasn't Devon."

His father's eyes narrowed. "Archer, don't lie to protect

him."

"I'm not lying." He glared at his father.

"I saw you go into the men's bathroom at seven . . . by yourself," he said.

"I left Devon for three minutes—five at the most." Archer's face turned red, and he wiped his forehead.

"You know that's more than enough time for Devon to pull this off. He's a master at four different styles of martial arts." He shook his head.

"That's right. And you know he's way too smart to leave fingerprints on a knife!" Lucy shouted.

"We don't think this was planned out. A crime of passion." Mr. Gallagher turned his accusing eyes toward me.

They thought this was my fault. "You think he killed him because of me?"

"Yes," one of the Elders answered.

"Well, there would be no reason. I didn't feel anything with Markus."

Mr. Gallagher eyed me. "He said you bonded, that you were his Soul Mate."

"He was wrong. Hasn't this happened before? Where one feels something, but not the other?"

"Not with Markus, or with any of the other Chosen Readers. The false positives have always been with the new Readers. It doesn't matter anyway, if Devon believed you were matched with Markus, it might've driven him to this. We'd have to be blind not to notice the chemistry between you two."

"Exactly. Devon is my match. We bonded, or whatever you call it, tonight. There wouldn't be a reason for him to kill Markus." My pulse hammered in a sporadic rhythm.

Lucy grabbed my hand and whispered, "Keep going. Try to talk them out of this."

"Why do you think I can hear his thoughts? No other Reader can hear him."

That stopped them for a minute. The guns lowered a little.

"Keep those guns on him. We'll be forced to shoot if he tries to escape," one of the Elders said.

Devon stood in the middle of the room with arms crossed and a dazed look, appearing too stunned to move.

"Even if that's true, it doesn't mean he knew it," Mr. Gallagher said. He motioned to the security men. "Let's go. We can address this at the tribunal."

Lucy ran to Devon and threw her arms around him. "No, you can't take him." Her panicked eyes pleaded with Archer. "Can't you do anything?"

"Dad. Please?" he asked.

"I'm sorry, son. He needs to go through the process just like everyone else."

Devon finally looked at me. I mouthed, "What do I do?" and he raised his shoulders. His sad eyes, those beautiful eyes I'd come to love, seemed to stare into my soul like it was the last time he'd see me.

"No!" I screamed. "I told you, Susie has something to do with this. Why won't you listen?"

"Enough," said another Elder. "We need to go into lockdown. Lucy, Archer, you're to go back to your rooms. We'll call for you to appear tomorrow."

"I won't go." Lucy stood next to her brother. "You can't make me."

"Please, Lucy. Don't make this worse," Devon said. "Go.

We'll work this out later."

*Oh, Devon. So calm and brave.*

Tears streamed down my face. I hadn't even noticed until I tasted the saltiness on my lips.

"Can I stay with Ann?" Lucy asked.

Archer's dad raised an eyebrow. "No. We don't want you to compare stories." He turned to a guard. "You'll need to stay here to protect Ann. I think the events tonight will trigger the war. We'll go into lockdown until we sort through all this."

I never told Lucy about my feelings. What would she tell them?

"I'll see you tomorrow," Devon said, looking at each of us. His eyes stopped when they met mine. "I'll come back to you. I promise."

"Okay. Okay," I repeated, not sure who I was trying to convince.

They left the room, all except for the armed security guard.

I shouted to Archer's dad, "I'm not going to leave. I'm going to stay right here and prove Devon had nothing to do with this." My body stood rigidly, hands clenched in determination.

I caught a glimpse of Devon's profile as he left. One of his half-smiles graced his lips.

"We'll see." Mr. Gallagher turned, motioned to Devon, and continued down the hall.

I examined my guard, knowing taking him down would be easy, but I spoke the truth to Mr. Gallagher. I wouldn't be leaving, not unless they took Devon from Samara.

They wouldn't do that, would they?

I stared at the guard for a few minutes. He stood straight, unmoving next to the door. I guess I needed to deal with this and form a plan. "As long as you have to be here, do you want coffee or something?" He glanced in my direction. "I'm not going to poison it or anything. You can watch me make it."

"No thanks, ma'am."

So formal. "You can call me Ann."

"Yes, ma' . . . Ann."

"That's better. You almost have it."

There would be lots of time to waste before the tribunal in the morning. Everything would be fine, I assured myself, pacing in front of the fireplace then around the room. He wasn't guilty, after all. I circled around the dining room table three or four times, adjusting the chairs. They don't prosecute innocent Readers. Back to the kitchen to look for some tea. Devon would be out soon, planning strategy against the Jacks.

Not finding the tea, I shuffled into the bedroom next. Anyone could put fingerprints on a weapon. Poor Markus, he didn't deserve to die. My sweats must be here somewhere. In a crouched position, I checked under the bed. Devon had to be upset to learn about his friend. Especially since they had just fought. I found the sweats, slipped them on, then returned to the main room. Devon's tough; he won't let them railroad him into a confession.

A book would be a good distraction. I grabbed one from the shelf, put it back, and picked up another.

"For God's sake, can you please stop?" the guard bellowed.

"What?"

His face contorted into a frown as he wiped his brow. "All this anxiety and pacing is driving me crazy. The tribunal won't be until tomorrow morning. Please, I beg of you, just sit down. Better yet, go to sleep. Time will go faster."

Eight hours later and I still paced, much to the chagrin of

my guard. I should've slept, but the adrenaline, combined with worry, made it impossible.

Two more hours and they called for me. Half asleep and wired up on two pots of coffee, I stumbled behind my escort into a large conference room. The fifty-two Elders peered at me from behind a large horseshoe table. I sat in a wooden chair in front of them.

I didn't care what it took; Devon would not be going to that prison.

I shifted in my seat and started. "Devon didn't—"

The Head Elder held up his hand. "We know what you think. We're only after the facts."

"What facts?"

"As you know, Markus was murdered last night." He clasped his hand together on the table. "As far as we can decipher, Devon is the only one with the motivation to commit this crime."

"No. Wait. I told you last night. Susie threatened to do something like this." They weren't listening to what I was telling them. Panic started low in my stomach.

"Susie has an alibi. She was in the Hub for the entire evening, with over a hundred people to confirm," he answered.

"Then she arranged it!" I stood, shaking. Had they already made up their minds?

"We know how you *feel*. But the evidence is conclusive." He slowly shook his head. "We wish it weren't so . . ."

"The evidence was staged."

"If that's the case, it will come out in the trial."

"You should also know I had a vision." I blurted out. The

room went silent. "This compound, well, it blew up. There was nothing left. Everyone died."

"When did you have this vision?"

"Right before Devon and I connected."

"We don't want to send him away. But we have a responsibility to protect the other Readers. Can you give us proof he didn't commit this crime?" he asked.

"He didn't murder Markus," I said. There was no doubt.

He lifted a brow. "And you know this because?"

"I just—I know, okay?" I stuttered out. This was not going well.

Fifty-two pairs of eyes stared at me, unconvinced.

"We need Devon to help fight the Jacks. Don't send him away now, not when you need him the most."

The Head Elder hesitated before speaking. "A few of the scenarios to defeat the Jacks involve you, not Devon."

I closed my eyes and let the words sink in. The plans involve me. That must mean, oh, no. "You want to use me as bait?"

"Yes."

"If I agree to this, you'll have to let Devon go. I know you believe he might be guilty, but he isn't. That's the only way I'll help you." I couldn't live in this world knowing Devon was locked away for a crime he didn't commit.

"You should know there is a chance you won't survive. There's a risk," he warned.

I nodded.

"We'll need to confer in private."

The group of Elders left the room in a single file. I sat back down in the chair. Had I told them enough? I'd just offered my life for Devon's freedom. The bond with him unbreakable, I'd do whatever was necessary to help him. I wrung my hands and tried to let courage be my guide. I could do this.

After a full hour, the Elders filed back into the room and sat down, their expressions somber.

"We have five possible plans. Are you willing to learn and practice each one?"

"Yes."

"As warned, two of the plans, specifically A and E, are ones where you won't make it out alive." He studied me, assessing my reaction.

I closed my eyes and lowered my head. My brain shut down, not wanting to comprehend it. I might have to leave Devon. My soul ached.

The Head Elder asked for a vote.

I glanced back up, held my breath and waited. Each held up a hand; it was unanimous. Devon would go free. I just hoped he'd forgive my decision.

Loud banging and an anguished cry came from down the hall.

"What's that noise? Are you hurting him?" A sharp pain pierced my chest.

"No. He's alone in a locked room down the hall. I think he may have heard you somehow." The Elders shifted in their chairs, shooting confused looks at each other.

I closed my eyes and covered my ears, unwilling to hear any more. Another vision swept in.

*Devon. He's holding a child in his arms, laughing and playing at the edge of an ocean beach, the waves lapping at his toes. He stops and points at the sunset then whispers into the child's ear and smiles.*

I spoke clearly. "Tell Devon I had another vision. He'll be happy again. Please tell him that's all I want. Also, that I'm sorry."

Committed to my decision, I left the room.

# CHAPTER 21

"WAKE UP!" STRONG HANDS gripped my shoulders, shaking them.

"Go away." I pushed off the offending hands interrupting my sleep. Between the worry, tribunal, and the hours of plotting against the Jacks with the Elders, I had nothing left. "I can't wake up."

"Ann, Ann! They lied. They've taken Devon." Archer took rapid breaths while continuing to shake me.

That did it. I shot up, clutching the blankets to me. "What do you mean . . . taken Devon?"

Archer rubbed his face. "I don't know if one of the Jacks got to an Elder. But my dad told me they've decided to take him to Colorado to deal with him there."

"They promised. They can't do that." The fog of sleep cleared, and anger began to build.

"They can, and they did. We have to stop them."

"Stop them how?"

"We have to get to him before they reach our Colorado facility. Once there, it'll be impossible to break him out. Hurry up."

"I am." I kicked the blankets off, jumped out of bed, and dashed for my closet. I grabbed a few items and asked, "What will I need?" I moved in slow motion, the shock messing with my brain.

"I don't care, but make it quick. We can get whatever else you need while we're on the road."

"What time is it? Is Lucy coming?" I grabbed the pillowcase from the floor and stuffed in the clothes I'd grabbed.

"It's four-thirty in the morning, Lucy's still in lockdown."

"How—"

"My dad." He let out a frustrated breath. "The perks of having an Elder for a father."

"I'm ready. We don't have to go through the tubes, do we?" The idea of it turned my stomach, but I'd do it if necessary.

"No. My access is still open. We can form our plan for Devon on our way."

"Okay. Let's go." I started for the door. "Wait." The kitchen drawer held the Kubotan Devon had given me. I grabbed it and followed Archer out.

Archer was right. We walked right down the halls, to the Jeep, and out of the compound, no problem. Once we were free, the anger exploded within me.

"I can't believe they took Devon. Do you think they lied to me from the start, hoping I'd go along with one of their plans for the Jacks?"

"My dad didn't tell me much. I just learned they planned to move him a few minutes before I came to you. Maybe they changed their strategy for the Jacks and didn't need you anymore." He waved to the guard as we passed through the entrance.

"Oh! That makes me furious." My body shook. *Oh, Devon. I thought you were safe.* But the vision . . ."We can still free him, right? Go into hiding? You two must know lots of places where we can disappear."

He smiled. "Of course, we can. And after the Readers win the war, we can come back and get everything straightened out."

"Will your dad be angry with you?" I worried about Archer risking his relationship with his father.

A shadow crossed his face. "Probably. My dad and I don't always see eye-to-eye." He cringed and kept his focus on the road.

"I'm sorry. I know your mom died protecting the Seers, just like Devon's parents. It must be hard to have a strained relationship with your last living relative."

He seemed to recover and gave a slight smile. "It could be worse."

"Yeah." Didn't I know it.

"As long as the truth comes out, it doesn't matter." Archer merged onto the main freeway, I-90 east, and turned on the radio.

I asked, "You aren't going to torture me with country music the entire trip, are you? Please, oh please, let me listen to something else, anything?" I put my finger on the button for my favorite station and waited.

Archer laughed, and his eyes crinkled in that charming way of his. "No, I'll spare you for this trip. Go ahead; you can pick. I'll even share some of my coffee with you."

I pushed the button. "You're a great friend, you know that?" I grabbed the thermos and poured myself a cup. I knew, with his help, we'd get Devon out of this mess.

"I feel the same about you." He turned up the radio and asked, "Top forty? Really?"

"Compromise? Soft rock?" I asked.

He pushed a button, and a soothing song started to play. I tried to entertain myself by looking out the window as the beautiful landscape whizzed by. I could see why my parents picked this area of the world to live.

"Do you think Susie could be a Jack? I know she's behind all this."

He shook his head. "Remember, she's been with us for thousands of years. Jacks don't have the luxury of existing in just one body. Susie would've had to switch her human form every thirty to fifty years."

"Even if she were, let's say, a mix of the two?"

His eyes cut over to mine. "What makes you ask that?"

"Doc said at the beginning, the races lived in harmony. He told me children were born from different races, sometimes watering down their abilities. If I'm the Lost One everyone seems to think I am, I'd have all three."

"Do you think you're the Lost One?" he asked.

"If I am, I haven't remembered yet. Right about now, I'd love to read some minds. Oh, and I'd also like to invade the Elders' thoughts and make them see reason. I still can't believe they went back on their word. I hope they'll investigate Susie."

"When you get your memory back, all your abilities will be restored."

"How can you be so sure?"

His shoulder lifted. "It's what I've heard from my dad and the Elders."

We had passed the freeway interchange exit. "Shouldn't we cut over and take the I-84?" I popped open the glove box and rifled around for a road map. "Wow. You're ready for any situation." Inside held handcuffs, a Taser, and mace.

He laughed. "You can blame Devon for those supplies. He stocked all our Jeeps with them last month."

Devon. Always thinking ahead.

"Anyway, we'll go I-90 to Idaho, cut through to Montana, and then we'll head south through Wyoming to Colorado. The Readers will most likely take the straight route, so this way we'll make sure to avoid them. It'll take a little extra time, but I know their routine. They always stop and rest for at least eight hours in Boise." He smiled. "We'll even have time to stop in Montana to rest and refuel for a few hours. There's a lodge outside of Helena, next to the most beautiful lake you'll ever see. A friend of mine runs it, and I visit whenever I can

"That's nice. I didn't think any of the Readers had friends outside Samara."

"We became friends years ago. Atarah is great. I think you'll really like her."

I wondered if Archer had feelings for this woman. No, he wouldn't waste time on a romantic rendezvous when Devon's life was at stake. But, still curious, I asked, "What's Atarah like?"

He smiled. "You'll see."

"You think we'll have time to visit, sleep, *and* get Devon free?"

"More than enough time."

I'd only had a few hours of sleep before Archer had shaken me awake earlier. I yawned and placed my head against the window and closed my eyes.

"Rest, Ann. You'll need your strength." He reached into the back seat, grabbed a blanket, and tossed it on my lap.

"You're an angel," I said before dozing off.

∽⚬⚜⚬∾

Hands shook me . . . again. I slapped them away. "Why do you keep doing that?" Ugh.

I sat up straight. Why was my brain so sluggish? I needed to be alert, not sleeping on the job. "Sorry, Archer. I'm a little out of it." The coffee I consumed earlier had done nothing for me. Terrible timing to be physically and emotionally drained.

"We're here. Come on, Atarah is waiting for us."

Why was he so focused on this Atarah person? Shouldn't we be planning our strategy for Devon? It was my fault, though. I'd slept most of the way.

I stretched out and asked, "What time is it?"

"We've been on the road eleven hours." He checked his watch. "It's three-thirty."

I stepped out of the Jeep and breathed in the fresh pine air. Gorgeous. "Wow." I swept my eyes around the landscape and resort. Rustic log cabins surrounded the large lake. There were so many of them, it was hard to guess the number. We'd parked in the lot with the main structure in front of us. Standing four stories tall, the log resort perched above the lake had extensive decks wrapping around the entire building. I turned slowly, taking in the stunning views of the lake, surrounding trees, water, stables and what appeared to be hiking trails. "No wonder you like to come here."

He let out a long breath. "I knew you'd like it."

"You must be tired. I'm so sorry I slept so much." Guilt ran through me. "I can drive the rest of the way." At least I hoped I could. I needed more caffeine.

"No need." He took my arm. "Come on, you'll love the lodge."

"It's huge. I wonder how many people it can hold."

"That one building over there can hold thousands of people. See over to the side?" He pointed to a massive building set off into the woods. "But the main building here will impress you most."

"I love all the decks." My mind, still foggy, tried to process something. It was at the edge of my memory, but I couldn't place it.

"It's time. Come on." He took my hand and led me up the steps. At the door, a lovely woman, about twenty-five years old, stood with her hands folded. Her wavy, brown hair cascaded down her back. She grinned at me through dark lashes.

Archer smiled at her and nudged me forward. "Here she is."

Had he told her about me?

"Welcome to the Lodge. I'm so excited to meet you. I've heard wonderful things. Come in, sit, have some tea." She beckoned me forward.

"So nice to meet you, Atarah." I reached out to shake her hand. Such an unusual name.

We walked into a three-story foyer with a huge chandelier made of antlers dangling from the ceiling. The lights cast an eerie glow throughout the room. It was open and spacious, but it somehow felt oddly cold for a log structure.

We passed through and entered a large reception room finished with warm beige and soothing cream colors. A huge, rock fireplace situated in the center held a roaring fire. This was better.

"Archer tells me you like tea." Atarah waved to a tea service set on a carved wood table. The teapot and matching cups were also carved from wood.

"This is a beautiful set. Is it handmade?" I asked. The fog had started to clear. I hoped the tea would help it along a little more.

Atarah smiled demurely and looked down. "Why, yes. It was carved by my Archer."

*My Archer.* Oh, so this was a romantic relationship like I suspected. I suddenly felt like the third wheel.

"Here, Ann. Sit right here." Archer guided me to one of the chairs next to the fireplace. It was a little different than the other furniture, metal with colorful pads that matched the rugged, mountain décor.

I sat, but before I had time to even blink, restraints snapped into place, binding my wrist to the metal arm of the chair.

# CHAPTER 22

"SHE'S QUITE ADEPT AT escaping. You'll need to make sure her other arm is immobile." Archer gave instructions to a security guard who entered the room. Or had the large man been there the entire time? I tried again to clear my head. This wasn't a sleep fog. The coffee. I'd been drugged.

"Devon is still at Samara, isn't he?"

He smiled at Atarah. "See, Mom? I told you she was smart."

"Mom?" I rasped. "She's your mom?"

The security guard fastened my other arm to the chair. I struggled, but . . . so sluggish. What had he slipped into my coffee?

*Two men. One can be trusted, the other not.* One of my first memories from the shore. Or had it been a voice? Why hadn't I listened?

"What's going on?" My head swung between Archer and his mom.

"Don't worry. Everything's going to be okay. I needed to

have you secure so you wouldn't be tempted to run off." He winked. "You know, when you get upset you like to do that." He smiled and patted my leg.

"How is everything going to be okay if I'm strapped to a chair?" I asked through gritted teeth.

Atarah came over and sat on the coffee table in front of me. "I know this is probably unsettling, but really, Archer is right. You'll love it here. It's so . . . serene." Her face lit up when she spoke.

"Are you a, uh, a Reader?" I asked.

"Oh, no!" She laughed and waved her hand in front of her face. "I'm a Jack," she said with a huge smile.

My breath caught, and I shivered, as though my blood had turned to ice.

"Mom, we need to give her information a bit at a time so she doesn't freak out. Look, she's shaking."

She picked up a bell from the table and rang it. A man dressed in a butler's uniform entered the room and bowed. "Yes, Ms. Atarah"

"I'll need a warm blanket." She took a closer look at me. "And a heating pad. Do we have one of those?"

"Yes, Miss Atarah." He bowed again and left the room.

"I'm so sorry." She rubbed my hand. "Oh, you do feel cold. I didn't mean to startle you. I know the Readers have a campaign to malign all the Jacks. Yes, it's true, some of the Jacks have given us all a bad name. But we're not all like that. It's like any community—a few bad apples." She shrugged.

"But, but . . . Archer is a Reader."

"Yes, by all appearances. But Archer is half Reader, half Jack. His DNA favors the Reader side, so he's probably fifty-one percent Reader. He's lucky, he doesn't have to change form like the rest of us.

My gaze turned back to Archer. "But, if you're more Reader than Jack, why are you here?"

Atarah's face scrunched into a frown. "His dad, always such a cold fish, judged poor Archer just because of his Jack blood. At least he never told any of the other Readers. Not for Archer's benefit, mind you. It was because he didn't want to lose his standing as the Head Elder. Even back then it was considered a poor choice to even talk to one of us. The Readers have always misunderstood us. He never really trusted you, did he?" she asked Archer.

He shook his head.

I wanted to say Archer proved his dad right, but kept it to myself.

She turned back to me. "The only good thing his dad did was to teach Archer and I to block properly. He's lived with the Readers all these years without one thought picked up by anyone. We're the only Jacks who've been able to master the technique." She smoothed her hair and continued. "Archer was never good enough for his father. After the war with the Seers, he sought me out, tired of all his dad's criticism. We hatched this plan thousands of years ago." She was back to smiling. "And here you are! All our hard work has paid off."

"If you knew where the compound was all this time, why didn't you move in earlier?"

"That was the beauty of our plan. We kept Samara's location limited to a small, select group. Some Jacks can be, what's the word I want? Oh yes, unpredictable. I worried they'd form a premature strike before you, the Lost One, showed up. The Seers had never made a mistake in their foretelling, so we patiently waited for your arrival." Atarah licked her lips like she'd just eaten a decadent piece of chocolate. Ugh. "Poor Archer had to live with those people for thousands of years."

A shadow of an emotion I couldn't pinpoint flashed in Archer's eyes.

Devon and the others needed to be warned. I struggled with my restraints, trying to be subtle about it so they wouldn't notice.

I said to Archer, "Uh, these fasteners are rather tight. I think I'm losing feeling in my hands."

Archer walked over to study my hands. He picked up each finger and massaged it. "We can't loosen them, not until you've heard everything about our plans. And your—well, we'll talk about that later. We'll untie you after you've been given the important details." He made a tsking sound. "Your fingers have enough circulation. Remember, I'm a doctor."

If he winked at me again, I'd scream.

The haziness cleared, and I searched around the room for a weapon. Archer would be a strong adversary, but I could most likely flatten his mother in thirty seconds or less. I'd only seen two other men so far. The Kubotan was tucked into my purse in the Jeep. Ugh. I examined my restraints. Made of Velcro, they were strong and tight. I twisted my wrists a little more. They wouldn't budge.

"So, Archer. You've lived with the Readers for thousands of years while planning their deaths?" I asked, trying to wiggle my wrists free.

His usual warm expression went dark. "Yes, it hasn't been easy." He rose and walked toward the floor-to-ceiling windows that highlighted the view of the lake and surrounding mountains. "But, one side has to die. Because of the Seer's vision, I was forced to choose. I can't lose my mom." He turned back to me. "You'll come to understand my decision. After it's done, we'll give you another wipe so you won't be burdened with these memories."

"It's true then. The Jacks—you—wiped my memory."

"Not me. We have a specialized team. As you've probably heard, we haven't perfected it yet."

"So you'll just give me some sort of memory wipe every year, is that your plan?" Not going to happen.

"No. We'll only need to do it once or twice. With the subjects we've been experimenting on, each time they have a wipe done, they remember less and less."

My right wrist loosened a little. If I could keep distracting them from my movement and the noise of the Velcro loosening, I'd be able to grab the glass candle holder and use it as a weapon. Once free, I could take down any attackers, hotwire the Jeep and get myself out of this place.

"How do you plan to kill the Readers?" I asked.

Atarah giggled, placing her hand over her mouth. "I'm sorry to be rude, dear. We can't give you that information. I like you, though. You have spunk."

The feeling was not mutual.

"She does. You should see her in action." He chuckled. "The Jacks knew you were most likely the Lost One after your parents published the article about you. We'd been tracking you for centuries. Your mom and dad had done a great job hiding you, but we sighted you on a rare outing about a year ago." He shook his head. "They were so careless. Thousands of years wasted because they wanted to take you to a small town fair."

"Why didn't you just take me then?" Their plan didn't make sense.

"We needed to make sure you were the Lost One before taking possession," Archer's mom said. "There've been mistakes in the past. We've almost been exposed too many times."

"I suspected it was you when you took Devon down during training." Archer chuckled. "Mom, you should have seen it. She was great."

Atarah nodded in agreement. "She's perfect."

They wouldn't think so for long. My fingers started to wiggle loose from the bindings.

"Anyway, I knew for sure when Markus arrived. After he tried to claim you, Devon fell apart. I knew at that moment it was you. The Seers predicted we'd all have a connection with you, and it's true. Devon never showed any real interest in the new Readers before you showed up."

Dread snaked through my body. *No.* "Archer," I whispered. "You didn't. You killed Markus?"

"Don't look at me like that. It was the only way. They all have to die anyway. Markus's time was just a little sooner."

"Devon and Lucy are your cousins and best friends. You'd kill them?" Numb with shock and disbelief, I remembered all the joking around, the movie nights, poker games, and long, philosophical discussions.

"Like I said, it's a tough choice, but I made it. I can't stop the war—it's been foretold." He turned to his mom. "I have to protect my mom. I'll do whatever it takes."

Archer had always been a yes man to his dad. Every time they were together, Archer was formal and polite. I should have realized something was off. That's probably why he'd turned into a mama's boy.

My hand was finally free. It was time. With lightning speed,

I picked up the metal chair and swung it as high as I could, aiming for Archer's temple. It connected on the side of his head, and, with a loud yelp and crash, he went down.

"Archer!" His mom raced to his side.

I grabbed the glass candlestick and crashed in on the side of the table. I ripped the other restraint from my arm. Freedom. I waved my new weapon at her. "Don't try to stop me." I swung it at her for good measure.

The words she spoke next froze me in place.

"Maybe you'd like to talk to your parents first?"

# CHAPTER 23

A SECURITY MAN RUSHED into the room.

"Winston, get some ice for Archer's head and bring Ann's parents to us," Atarah demanded.

"You're bluffing." I gripped the broken candlestick, ready for battle.

"They're already here, Ms. Atarah," Winston said.

I braced myself and turned. The two people from my vision on the beach, who they wanted me to believe were my parents, stood hand-in-hand by the entrance. They were a little different, maybe older, but there was no mistaking their identity. I recognized them from my flashback.

"Ann." The woman put her hand to her mouth.

The reaction I had this time was even stronger. My makeshift weapon dropped from my hand, shattering the glass table then tumbling to the floor. I gasped for air, not able to get enough. Flashing dots swirled before my eyes, threatening a blackout.

The couple moved toward me, but I put up my hand to stop them.

This could be a trick. These people—imposters.

*Get it together, Ann.*

I asked Atarah. "How do I know they're really my parents? They could be part of your memory wipe, their picture implanted into my memory somehow." I turned to the couple and asked, "Did you know they've wiped my memory?"

"We know." Tears ran down the woman's face.

"Do you have any memories of us?" The man stood rigid, waiting for my response.

"Just the picture of you. That's all. No memories."

His narrowed eyes landed on Atarah. "You said she wouldn't be hurt."

She held ice to Archer's forehead. "As I've told you, Mr. Baker, it will take another six to ten months for it to wear off. She's not hurt, but look what she's done to my poor Archer."

The woman, who could possibly be my mom, shot a slight grin and subtle nod my way.

"Will you answer some questions for me?" I asked.

"Of course, anything," the man responded.

"Tell me, what was our favorite movie to watch?" I asked the woman.

Without hesitation, she said, "*Pride and Prejudice.*"

Archer moaned and turned over.

"Oh, thank goodness, you're okay." Atarah placed her hand on Archer's forehead then sent a glare my way. Yeah, I knew her friendliness would be short-lived.

I ignored her and asked the man, "What was our favorite

dinner?"

"Spaghetti."

"And . . ." I coaxed.

"Meatballs." He wiped a tear.

My mom clapped her hands together. "You do remember some things."

"No, sorry. I don't remember, but I was told about it." *Devon. The day on the river.*

Their smiles and bright eyes gave way to slumped shoulders and a disappointed "Oh."

I walked to stand in front of them. "But I believe you."

They each took one of my hands, and a comforting warmth swept through me. I had my parents back.

My mom whispered in my ear, "You have powers, Ann. The memory wipe has made you forget them. Tap into it. You're going to need them."

"What are you whispering about over there? No more talking until after the union," Atarah said.

Union? That couldn't be good.

Archer groaned again, taking her attention off us for a moment.

I asked my mom, "Do you know what she's talking about?"

"Yes. They seem to think, if you marry a Jack, it will override the soul mate requirement. They have some High Priest or something to do the ceremony."

"Marry a Jack?" Archer? Or someone else? It didn't matter who they chose. I wouldn't go along with it.

My mom noticed my expression and said, "I'm so sorry, Ann. They plan to use us as leverage to get you to go along with their plans."

"I'll get us all out. How much security do they have here?" My mind raced with possible plans to escape.

"They don't need security for us." Mom shook her head and held out her arm, revealing an ominous small lump above her wrist which made me uneasy. "They implanted your dad and me with a poison. If you try to remove it, it will release and kill us. They can also trigger it remotely." She glanced back at Atarah. "If it means you can get away and save the Readers, I want you to escape. No matter what happens to us."

My father added, "We've talked about this, Ann. We're prepared to die to save you and the other Readers."

"No! There has to be a way to save all of us." I had to find a way.

"Our purpose has always been to protect you. If we can get you free, that's all we want."

My mom took my hand. "It's my fault you're here, that we're all here in this place."

"What do you mean?"

"We'd hidden you for thousands of years, and tried to make a normal life for you at the same time. But it wasn't normal. I'm sorry they took your memory, but some things . . ." Her sad eyes met mine. "You've been through a lot. Things I wouldn't have chosen for you. You're special, remember that."

"It's okay. I understand." The need to reassure overcame my feelings of loss.

"I hoped for just one carefree day for you. That's all, one day at the fair." She hugged me. "I wanted you to experience some fun."

"It was a great day." My dad smiled. "I think you did a hundred loops on the Ferris wheel."

"That sounds like fun." I didn't want my mom to feel bad, but I had an idea of what had happened.

She nodded. "Somehow, the Jacks spotted us. We'd been on their radar for hundreds of years." She took a deep breath. "We didn't know about it until it was too late. We thought we were safe. They began to track us. That's when we published the article, hoping the Readers would find you first."

"You didn't know where the Readers were?"

"We lost contact with them after the war. We had no way of finding them. As you know, they've stayed hidden away from the rest of the world. We knew about the Seers vision and had hoped the Readers would find us before the Jacks." She glanced over at Archer and Atarah. "But before we could make contact, the Jacks stormed our house. They grabbed you before I could hide you away." Her cheeks turned red. "I hated putting you in that place, especially after the incident with the rat."

Oh. The rat. I wouldn't tell her the coffin-like hiding place was one of my only memories to come through. She had enough guilt.

"Enough talking," Atarah said. "They've filled you in about the poison?"

Archer had gained consciousness and was propped on the couch, listening to our conversation.

"Yes. I know what you've planned."

"The sooner you come to terms with it the better." Her brow lifted. "Unless, of course, you want your parents to die?"

# CHAPTER 24

*I* *LOVE YOU. I'LL find you no matter what it takes.*

My eyes shot open, and I gasped for breath. I clawed at the thing wrapped around my neck, choking me.

Sheets. They had twisted around while I slept. I pushed the sweaty, matted hair from my face, calmed myself, and glanced around. I'd been too tired to notice the night before, but the bedroom they put me into—or locked me in—was ghastly. How old did they think I was, five? Pink walls, pink furniture, with a platform bed and a frilly, pink canopy. If I didn't die from sugar-sweet overload, the pink sheets would finish the job.

It was Devon's thoughts that woke me, I was sure of it. I squeezed my eyes shut and thought . . . I love you, too. I'll come back to you, hoping he'd hear me. Not likely though.

Think.

I threw the blankets to the side and stepped onto the stool to get off the ridiculous bed. A silvery light came from the window across the room. I pulled the curtains back, and, sure enough, someone had installed bars to keep me in. But they didn't need them. I didn't have my memories, but they weren't able to steal the love I had for my parents. The Jacks couldn't take that from me, even though they'd taken everything else. They had me at their mercy . . . for now.

A tap on the door alerted me to Archer's arrival. After he entered, he turned and spoke to the guard at my door. "I'll knock when I'm done." He closed the door and gave me a slight smile. He wore a bandage where I'd struck him. My eyes darted around the room, searching for another weapon.

"Don't bother. This room has been stripped clean. You won't find anything."

"Figures," I said under my breath.

"What?"

"Never mind. What is all this?" I gestured to the room.

He smiled with the same warmth we had as friends. My stomach sank. He wasn't the sweet, funny Archer I believed he was. Tears started to fill my eyes, but I blinked them away. There wasn't time to grieve for the friend I'd lost.

"My mom went a little overboard." He motioned to the couch. "Here, I want to talk to you about what's going to take place."

I ignored my urge to punch him and sat down. It wouldn't hurt to get as much information as possible. Play nice, I reminded myself.

He touched his bandage. "I don't blame you for this."

That was good. I didn't blame me either.

"I understand how hard this is. It wasn't supposed to happen this way." He studied his hands.

"What do you mean?"

"We were supposed to take custody of you at your parents' house. Remember? After the radio broadcast when you left the first time?"

I closed my eyes and let the realization sink in. "It was you, not Susie, who staged the broadcast."

Obnoxious Susie was just that. Not the devious, lying killer I believed she was.

"Yes, and if Devon hadn't barged in to save the day, I wouldn't have had to kill Markus to get you from the compound. It's his fault." He scowled.

He was delusional. I rubbed my temples. "It doesn't make sense. Why couldn't you just have kidnapped me or something?"

He pointed to his injured head. "We had to make sure, when you left Samara, it was your idea. You've barely scratched the surface of your talents. We know what you're capable of, and that meant we had to be creative to get you to leave."

"The gunshots at the beach?"

"Jacks. Only to scare you into coming with us."

I'd played right into their hands.

I got up from the couch and walked back to the window. The sun had just started to rise. "Can you tell me anything about what's going to happen to me and my parents?"

He came and stood next to me. After adjusting his tie and smoothing his hair, he blurted,

"I'm in love with you."

What? "No, you aren't." I shook my head to add emphasis.

"I assure you, I am. Desperately, in fact."

"Why?" I asked, pretty sure my brain had clicked off.

"See? Right there. You've no idea how beautiful you are. But it's not your beauty I love. It's you, Ann. I love everything about you. Your sense of humor, the way you're so fearless, yet vulnerable. When you love someone, you do it with your heart and soul. That's why we had to use your parents. We knew it'd be the one thing that would stop you from running off. Even without your memories, your love for them is unwavering." He tugged at the bars on the window. "I don't even think we need these, do we?"

My shoulders slumped. "No."

"I know you won't allow yourself to love me now, but . . . after the memory wipe, everything will be fine. I'll earn your love. I promise I'll make you happy."

Don't freak out. "So, you're who I'm supposed to be joined with in the union?"

"Yes. On Saturday."

"Five days from now?" That didn't give me enough time.

He smiled. "Yes, Ann. I know this must be a shock, but after all these unpleasant memories are gone, you and I will have a great life together. Do you remember how much fun we had?" His eyes searched mine. I tried to keep my expression blank. "We still need to have another chess rematch. I plan to win one of these days."

Great. He wanted to wipe my memory and play chess.

"When do you plan to do this wipe?" Please don't let it be today.

"After our union. The High Priest insists. This way, we'll have some shared memories together. He'll use them to bind our spirits together forever. I know it will make the union ceremony harder for you, but I promise, as soon as it's over,

I'll make sure they do the wipe right away."

Not comforting.

"This plan started for me as a way to help the Jacks win the war. But now, it's all about you." He took a step toward me. But I moved back. "I want to be near you all the time, and when I'm not, I feel lost." His eyes filled, and he reached a hand out to me.

Oh, no you don't.

Another knock at the door interrupted us. Atarah breezed in, carrying a tray of food. "Oh, look at you two. Awake and ready to start your day. Ann, I've brought you some breakfast. Archer told me your favorite is egg white omelet with dry toast. It sounds too healthy for me," she said with a laugh.

My stomach churned.

She said to Archer, "Will you excuse us, dear? Ann and I have some details about the union that need to be discussed."

He examined the tray with my food.

"It's all plastic, the rubbery kind you can't break," Atarah reassured him.

Appetizing. Rubber plates and utensils.

Archer's eye focused on mine. "Please, think about what I've told you. Things will be good again. You'll have your parents back."

But not Devon or Lucy. Or any of the Readers. I missed our compound in the mountain. I wanted—no, I needed them back.

We've left Samara. The Elders said go to plan E. Another thought from Devon.

I froze in the middle of the room. The thought—those words. Did I hear them right?

Plan E?

Oh, no. That meant—that meant I wouldn't see Devon again.

Devon. Please, God. No.

I bent forward, placing my hands on my legs, and took in large gulps of air. If Devon knew what plan E entailed, I didn't think he would have told me. That was one of the plans I'd practiced with the Elders before Archer had whisked me away.

The plan where I wouldn't make it out alive.

"Archer, what's wrong with Ann? She looks like she might faint." Atarah moved a little closer to examine me.

"Ann, are you having a panic attack?" Archer asked.

I couldn't look up at them, not yet. "No. I'll be okay in a minute." I waved them off.

The Elders wouldn't have sent the message if there had been any other alternative. Now that the Jacks had me, it made sense. I went over the details in my mind. It could be done, but there would be some big hurdles.

I sat back down on the couch and pulled myself together. "I'm fine now."

Not.

I asked Atarah, "You have some things you wanted to talk to me about?"

Archer reached over, took my pulse, and laid his hand on my forehead. "Whatever it was seems to have passed."

"You go on now. I'll take good care of her." She smiled sweetly.

Ugh.

"Thanks, Mom. I know you will." With one last searching

look my way, he left the room.

She placed the tray on the coffee table in front of the sofa and sat next to me. "We got off to a bad start yesterday. I'm sorry I became angry with you."

You're not sorry. You don't care about anyone but yourself. A new voice, one I hadn't heard before.

I watched her mouth carefully, but it hadn't moved. Oh my, I could read her thoughts. I guess her blocking technique wasn't as airtight as she thought. But why would she be thinking that about herself?

Then, it hit me—no way! I wasn't reading her thoughts; they were from the human body she'd stolen. Their souls didn't leave like the Readers thought. No wonder their intelligence dropped fifty percent in some cases. How could a person function like that? It took every bit of energy left in my body to cover my shock.

Shut up. You have as much to lose if this doesn't go as planned. We both die if the Readers get her back, thought Atarah.

You're wrong. I'm already dead, the other voice said.

Do I need to torture you again? You know I'll do it, she said to the other soul.

Atarah smiled, like her only goal was to make me comfortable.

"As I was saying, let's put the unpleasantness behind us. We have lots to plan before Saturday." She placed a napkin on my lap.

The other voice remained quiet. What type of torture would threaten her without also hurting Atarah?

"Okay." I nodded. How would I possibly fake my way through this one?

"The High Priest will arrive today. Whatever your feelings are about us, you'll need to respect him. He'll perform the binding-of-the-souls at the ceremony."

"Is he a Jack?" I asked.

"Of course. He holds the highest rank and has the most power."

I prepared myself for the next question. With sweaty palms clasped together, I asked, "Where will the ceremony be held?"

"Here, of course. We have Jacks flying in from all around the world."

It was now or never. I focused on her face, keeping my expression bland. Concentrate. The Readers know your location. I sent the thought to Atarah.

She frowned and a slight crease formed between her brows.

I continued my concentrated thought. Go to a place they'd never suspect.

Atarah stood up and said, "I need to go make more arrangements." She walked to the door and stopped. "I'll be back with the dress for your fitting in a few hours."

"Can I leave my room? You have my parents, so . . ."

Ann needs to bond with her parents to keep her in line. I hoped this thought worked, because I needed to talk to them.

She addressed the guard. "She can leave, but make sure you follow her. I'm giving my permission for her to talk to her parents. It'll give Ann more incentive to cooperate if they get some more bonding time." She cocked her head to the side and narrowed her eyes. "I think you know me well enough by now to know I'd have no problem killing your parents if you try to escape."

"You are an evil, conniving witch," the other voice, the one I was beginning to like, came through.

Serves her right inhabiting someone who hated her so much. I bit my tongue and said, "Yes, I understand."

# CHAPTER 25

"CAN YOU LEAD ME to my parents' room?" I asked the guard after Atarah left my room.

*His eyes did one of those up and down body scans. Yeah, baby. I'll take you to places you've never been before.*

His lips hadn't moved, so I didn't acknowledge his rude comment.

Instead, he said, "Sure, follow me. They're in one of the cabins on the east side of the lake."

An average guy, around twenty-years-old with a strong, muscular build. He wore a uniform like the other guards, but his patch told me he was a supervisor. It should have read, 'Pig.'

*Why should Archer get her? Don't you think it's unfair? If you kill Archer, you're next in line,* another voice said.

I was getting his other soul's thoughts, too?

*I do as I'm told. If you had your way, I'd be in prison right now,* the guard answered back.

*I am in prison, so why shouldn't you be, too?*

Wow. No wonder the Jacks were a miserable bunch. Once out the front door, I sucked in some fresh Montana air. My shoes crunched on the gravel as we headed toward the path that wound around the lake.

The guard stopped in front of one of the small log cabins that dotted the shoreline. Everything about this place was a contradiction. Quaint and charming tucked in around selfishness and greed. Had my parents been able to shield themselves from the negativity of the Jacks? Exhaustion and a headache drained me after just a few minutes in their company.

The cabin door flung open, revealing Mom. "Ann!" She took me in long hug.

I wondered briefly why I didn't feel awkward, but warmth and love radiated from her like a comforting blanket. I hung on for an extra beat, savoring the moment.

She grasped my hand. "Come in."

I stepped across the threshold and took in the surroundings. Hand-carved log furniture, an old-fashioned wood-burning stove, and a delightful little kitchen and dining set filled the living area. "Well, at least you've had a nice place to stay."

"Yes, the beauty doesn't match the people who live here."

I smiled. "I was just thinking the same thing." We stood for a second longer, eyes connected, enjoying the moment.

My dad sat a few feet away, working on a jigsaw puzzle. He looked up and smiled, dropping his puzzle piece. I smiled back, relieved they had at least a little normality.

"We need to talk," Mom said.

"Is it safe to talk here? Could it be bugged?" I asked.

"Most definitely." She gestured to my dad, and we left the cabin, starting on the path bordering the lake. The guard followed close behind.

"I can read some of the Jacks thoughts, can you?" I asked in a low voice.

"Yes. I hoped you'd retain some of your abilities." My mom put her hand over her heart. "I'm so relieved. You'll be much better equipped to make your escape. You can also influence their thoughts. Have you tried that yet?"

"A little, but I'm not sure if I got through."

"Keep trying." Her eyes shifted around the area. "We used to order products from Amazon so you could practice on the UPS delivery person. You'd have them drop and pick up the package at our door fifty times before letting them leave." She chuckled. "They probably wondered the next day why they were sore."

"Oh." I covered my mouth to stifle a giggle. "That wasn't nice of me."

"They were fine. Exercise is good for a person." She laughed.

I turned to check on the guard's position. He appeared bored and was looking out onto the lake.

"I want to tell you about your history. You'll need more information about your talents." Mom kept her voice low. "I'm half Reader, half Jack. And your Dad is half Reader, half Seer."

"Wow." I couldn't think of anything else to say.

"It's limited our powers in some ways. But the fact you have all three has enhanced your abilities up by at least ten-fold. We've been training you for centuries."

I smiled. "That's how I knew how to hot wire a car?"

Mom grinned. "Among many other things. When the time came, we wanted you to be prepared."

"The two of you would practice talking together telepathically. Sometimes I'd feel left out of the conversation." My dad chuckled.

The inner voice. "Mom! Were those messages from you? I kept hearing a voice at the beginning."

Her face lit up. "Did they get through?"

"Yes. I couldn't figure it out. I thought I was going crazy." My stomach sank. "I pushed your voice away. I think I actually said 'Shut up.' I'm so sorry, Mom."

"I heard. I knew about the mind-wipe, so I kept trying. Unfortunately, I didn't know Archer was the Jack at first. I tried to get the information to you later, but I think you had closed yourself off by then."

I'd probably missed a lot of important information about the Jacks. Well, no time like the present.

"Can you tell me a little more about the Jacks? How did they pull off faking your murder?" I asked.

"They caused the fire, as you probably know. They replaced our bodies with two homeless people. They gave them a place to stay and told them they'd have jobs." She took my hand again. "These Jacks are terrible people." Her brow wrinkled, and she shot a glance at the guard.

"I know."

"They removed their teeth so police couldn't identify them." She shuddered.

My dad rubbed her shoulder. "It's okay. You don't have to talk about this now."

Her jaw clenched then released. "No. She needs this information. It'll help her."

Atarah might decide we can't talk anymore." With a sigh, she continued, "They took out a back molar from both of us and placed it at the scene for DNA identification."

"That's horrible." My stomach churned.

"Yeah, they planned it well," my dad answered.

"They wanted you to be suspected of the crime. The wipe would make you appear to be guilty. Archer and Devon were meant to break you out of police custody, but you beat them to it." He smiled.

"The Jacks hired some old sea captain and his first mate to locate you after you were shot by the police. Their instructions were to dump you on Lopez Island. They wanted you with the Readers until they could discern if you were the Lost One. That's how Archer knew where to find you. It was all set up from the beginning."

I let the new information sink in and asked, "What about this union they plan. Will it really replace the bond I already have with Devon?"

"What? You bonded with Devon?" Mom's eyes widened as she stopped and grabbed my shoulders. "Did it happen?"

"I hope that's a good reaction because, yeah, we bonded— like, crazy, tip-the-world-on-its-axis bonding." I smiled. But my heart sank, when I remembered the Elders' plan.

"It is! I had hoped for Devon. His parents were so brave and honorable. I knew he was one of the four chosen from the Seer's vision, but I could only dream." She hugged me tight. "This is the best news."

"I do have a little bad news, though." How would I tell my mom about the plan when she was filled with hope? I swallowed hard, hesitant to tell them the awful truth. "I heard one of Devon's thoughts just before I came." I bit my lip, pulling together all the courage I could muster. "The Elders want me to go to Plan E. We had discussed five plans, but, because of my disappearance, I think they've figured out that the Jacks have me."

"What's Plan E?" my dad asked.

If I told them, they might try to interfere. The Elders' instructions were precise, and I'd follow them like we'd practiced back at Samara. *We've constructed a fingerprint detonation bomb. We can't risk a remote device. The Jacks have sensors that would disarm it before ignition. We'll program the bomb so you'll be the only one who can set it off.*

I took a deep breath. "It's one of the five plans in which I don't survive."

"No!" they both shouted.

The guard approached us with narrowed eyes. "What's going on here? What's with the yelling? This was supposed to be a happy family reunion or something."

"It is." I smiled. "I squashed a bug on my arm, and they got upset. You know how vegetarians are with their 'protect-all-life' philosophy." What was I saying? It wasn't even a good lie.

"I don't care if you kill a cow. If I hear anymore yammering out of you three, we head right back for the lodge. You hear me?" He stood with arms crossed.

"Yes, sir," I said. He fell back into position, and I continued talking to my parents in a lowered voice. "I knew it was a possibility when I had the meeting with the Elders. If I'm able to rid the world of the Jacks and make sure Devon and the rest of the Readers live, I can deal with it. I'm all right, really."

Mom's lip trembled, and she took rapid breaths.

I hugged each one to reassure them. "Your job was to protect me. But my destiny is to protect the Readers. It'll be okay."

"What are the details of the plan?" my dad asked.

"Part of my agreement with the Elders is to never speak of the plan." I lowered my voice even more. "A precaution, but it's probably not a bad idea. If I can accomplish what I need, there'll be some changes, so can you go with the flow? I'll try to warn you right before."

We'd walked about a half-mile when the guard's communicating device beeped. He removed it from his waistband. "Yes. I understand. I'll bring her right away."

The guard approached us. "We'll need to get back to the lodge. The High Priest has arrived."

The trek back was silent and somber. My parents' expressions were both sad and resigned. The vision of Devon on the beach with a child in his arms gave me a sense of peace. It also filled me with sadness to know it most likely wasn't our child, and another woman would take my place. I turned away and wiped the stray tear that had escaped. He'd live and love again. He'd be happy. It was enough. It had to be.

*Sometimes you have to fight for love.*

"Mom? Was that you?"

She smiled and said, "Keep your eyes open."

I hugged her back. "I love you."

I watched my mom and dad walk hand-in-hand back into their cabin.

Now, I needed to get to work. First up, the guard escorting me back to the lodge. I concentrated my thoughts and focused on him.

*The Readers know the location of the lodge. They plan to attack on Saturday.*

He became rigid, stopping right before we started up the steps. His head swung from side to side, perhaps looking for intruders.

*The Readers are on their way. You must leave.*

"Come with me. Hurry." He wiped his brow and started up the stairs. Once inside, the guard greeted Archer and his mom. "May I approach the High Priest? I have news."

The group turned to look at me. I played innocent and shrugged.

"Does this have anything to do with Ann?" Archer asked.

"No. It's about the Readers."

The man, who was no doubt the High Priest, stood across the room and examined our group with an intense, penetrating stare. He appeared to be around eighteen years old, wearing an elaborate white robe with intricate stitching and lace.

What caught my attention, though, was the three-foot-tall, stiff, white hat perched on his head. For goodness' sake, could he be any more unoriginal?

The Pope wannabe sauntered over to our group. He gave a slight nod, as if I were below his rank. "Miss Baker."

"Hey."

Archer and Atarah went still and stared at me with their wide eyes. I guess that wasn't respectful enough for them.

"You may call me High Priest Cyneric."

"Sure thing," I said. I'd be pushing a few of his buttons before this was said and done. Who said I couldn't go out in a blaze of glory and bring him down a few notches at the same time? And, right now, it gave me great satisfaction to watch his pompous face turn red.

Atarah spoke. "I'm sorry, Your Most Holy. She has been out of sorts since her arrival."

An understatement.

Time to get into that pontifical head of his. I focused on him and thought over and over. *This place has negative energy. The union cannot be performed here.*

The guard approached. "High Priest Cyneric, I have news."

"You may speak."

"I've been told the Readers know of our location and are planning an attack on Saturday. We must evacuate as soon as possible."

He breathed in deeply and said, "Yes, I felt it. What are our alternatives?"

"What do you mean?" Atarah burst out. "Everything is planned. The entire Jack community is either on their way or will be in a matter of hours."

His nostrils flared. "I said, this place won't do."

Atarah folded her hands and cast her eyes to the floor. "I beg your forgiveness, Your Most Holy."

Again, I focused my energy on the High Priest's thoughts. *A place where Ann was happy.*

"For the spiritual bonding to take hold, Miss Baker needs an environment where she's comfortable."

Wow. I almost believed the thought came from him.

Atarah rubbed her forehead. "We can't go back to her family home. There isn't enough room. The Seers' vision said the bond had to be witnessed by every single Jack."

"I know what the Seers predicted," he bellowed.

She drew back and stood behind a quiet Archer.

"She was comfortable at Samara," Archer said. "And the reports said the Readers scattered once they found out we were both gone." He rubbed his jaw. "I can gain access even if they changed the codes. I was the one who programmed it."

The High Priest turned to me. "Is it true? Were you comfortable there?"

"Yeah, I guess."

Archer's expression didn't change. Was he suspicious about the possible change of venue?

The High Priest clapped his hands. "It's settled. We'll move the ceremony there. Alert all the Jacks who've started their travels so they can reroute."

"I'll get on that." Archer left the room.

Now, how to get Atarah to go along? Yes, that might work. Focus. *The bonding ceremony will take place in their precious Samara, right under their noses.*

Atarah stiffened and tapped a finger against her lips. Her eyes darted to me and narrowed.

My face remained perfectly bland as I met her stare. I could control that, but my heart almost pounded out of my chest.

I concentrated with everything in me. *I'll show those Readers who's won.*

Atarah smiled and said. "I love the idea of having the ceremony in the Readers' beloved home."

# CHAPTER 26

O N THE TRIP BACK to North Bend, I asked Archer, "Where will the ceremony be held? In the Hub?"

"That's the plan. We won't be able to fit everyone in there, so we'll have live links broadcast into all the other rooms. Only the higher dignitaries will get placement in the Hub."

"Who are they?"

"Jacks who've risen through the ranks either through their original birthright or by . . ." He paused and tapped his fingers on the steering wheel.

"What?"

"By how many Readers they've been able to kill."

"That's . . . that's horrible." I rubbed my eyes. Would this car ride ever end?

"It's the way it is. Remember, you're part Jack, just like me."

"Just because you have Jack blood doesn't make you a bad

person. Your choices in life define who you are." I was living proof. I had Jack blood running through my veins, but I'd never be like them.

"I regret it." He glanced over at me from the driver's side of the Jeep.

I didn't acknowledge him.

"Markus. I regret what I did."

"Why? You plan to kill all the rest. What difference does killing Markus make?" The bitterness came through.

"I would change everything if I could. My mom and I had this plan for thousands of years, and I've been caught up in it. After I met you, things started to change. *I* changed. But it was too late. I didn't know how to switch sides. And . . . I couldn't let my mom die. I want both of you to live."

"You made your choices a long time ago, Archer." I turned away.

I didn't speak to him for the rest of the car ride. I couldn't fathom the prospect of receiving another mind-wipe and living in ignorance for the rest of my life. Cold fingers of fear crawled up my spine. No, not going to happen.

⚜

Bittersweet. I was home, at the compound, but it wasn't the same. The heart was gone, replaced with teeming insects that called themselves Jacks. They were everywhere, and with them, emptiness had replaced the happiness.

When I lived with the Readers, there were three-hundred-forty-three of us. Now, over five thousand Jacks crammed into Samara. Three-hundred-fifty-thousand square feet built into the mountain. Impressive, but now overcrowded.

Somehow Archer had arranged for my parents and me to share my old room in an attempt to make me feel more "comfortable," something considered important by the High Priest. What a joke.

"Ann, honey, can I get you anything?" my mom asked.

"Just something so I don't throw up on Atarah when she comes for the dress fitting."

"That woman drives me crazy, and I'm not even plagued with reading her thoughts. There's some poetic justice in the fact the Jacks can't fully rid themselves of the souls they've captured."

"Yeah, well, try reading her thoughts. It's a mess in there."

"Your talent shouldn't be wasted on them." Her gaze was unblinking for a moment, almost as if she were trying to form an alternate plan. I knew this couldn't happen. This was my destiny.

I needed to distract her. "So, the Readers can pick up the Jacks thoughts, but only from the dominant soul?"

"All this time, we believed the Jacks killed their human's soul. Your discovery is quite the revelation. I doubt there's anything you can't do." She smoothed my hair back. "Ann . . ."

"There isn't any other way, Mom."

The door burst open. "I'm here with your beautiful dress!" Atarah announced.

Hideous. I should have guessed after seeing the atrocious room she prepared for me at the lodge. The thing was stiff enough to stand on its own. A confection of white lace and frills, it spanned about ten feet wide and twenty long.

After dragging it in, she held it up with reverence, like it was some holy artifact. I took it from her hands and pulled it into the bathroom after me. If I could flush it down the toilet, I would. But I reminded myself to play along in order to carry out the plan.

My mom came to help me into it. Once she had it zipped, our eyes met in the mirror. A marshmallow covered in lace and sequins was the best way to describe me. I put my hand over my mouth, and we broke into uncontrollable giggles.

"It's absurd!" My mom wiped her eyes.

Pain and hilarity pulled at my emotions. I hugged her through the frills. "Thank you, Mom. Thanks for making me laugh when, well, this moment could have been bad."

"What's going on in there?" Atarah pounded on the door. "You better not be doing anything to that dress. It cost over two hundred thousand dollars!"

"No way," I said, and we burst into another round of hilarity. Maybe it was nervous laughter, but I didn't care. At the end, I hugged her and said, "Thanks again, Mom."

"I wish . . ."

"I know." We both wiped tears of laughter and sadness from our eyes.

We joined Atarah and her seamstress in the living room. "Look at that—it fits perfectly." The seamstress clapped her hands.

*That is the most God-awful dress I've ever seen,* Atarah's bothersome human roommate thought.

I bit the inside of my cheek in an effort to stop myself from agreeing with her.

*Shut up. After this is over, I'll make sure you pay for trying to interfere with me,* Atarah thought.

*I'm tired of your threats. Maybe I'll find a way to take over and tell Archer you're not his real mother.*

My eyes darted up to her, and she caught me staring. I needed to cover. "What shoes will I wear?"

She didn't answer and studied me.

*She knows,* the human soul thought.

"You are not to see Archer before the ceremony," Atarah said.

I shrugged. "I hadn't planned on it."

*She doesn't know. You're only trying to cause trouble, as usual,* Atarah scolded the human.

I let out a sigh. That was close. I grabbed my mom, scurried into the bathroom to remove my dress, and slipped on a pair of sweats and a t-shirt.

I left the dress hanging over the shower rod and moved back into the living room, where I continued my bluff and asked the seamstress, "Are these shoes all right?" I held up the flats I'd been wearing.

She dismissed my comment with a wave of her hand. "Yes, that'll be fine. They won't show anyway."

After they left, I grabbed my mom by the shoulders. "You'll never believe this, but that's not even Archer's mom. She's a fraud!"

"What?" Her mouth dropped open.

"I heard them arguing right before they left. I can't believe it. How do you think she pulled it off?"

"Jacks always have to change their form. She probably got all the information about Archer from his real mom. For all we know, she could've murdered the real Atarah to set up this entire thing. I'll tell you, every single one of those Jacks are ruthless."

"Should I tell Archer? I guess it doesn't matter now. But his life is based on a lie."

"Tell me what?"

I turned and came face-to-face with Archer.

My heart began to race. "How'd you get in here?"

"I'm programmed in, remember? What did you mean, my life is a lie?"

I steadied myself. "You've done all this . . ." I gestured around. "For an imposter. She's a Jack posing as your mom. She might have even murdered your real mother. I heard her. I can read her thoughts."

"No." The color drained from his face as he digested my words. "I would know something like that."

"Can you read her thoughts?" I asked.

"No, we both can block. But, even without that, because I'm half Reader my powers aren't as strong." He rubbed the back of his neck.

"Have you ever doubted her?" I asked. There had to have been slips along the way.

"Sure. But I always believed her memory lapses were due to the change from body to body. But . . ." He stared down at his hands.

"You remember something?"

He met my eyes. "It can't be. How long ago would it have been?"

"The switch probably took place during the war. It was a confusing time for all of us," my mom said.

He frowned and rubbed his forehead. All the little doubts must be creeping back in.

The door swung open again. "There you are, Archer. I've been looking all over for you." Atarah turned toward me, shaking her forefinger. "Ann, you naughty girl. I told you no visiting until the union." She noticed our expressions. Her faced reddened. "She's lying. Don't trust anything she says!"

Archer turned slowly and faced her. "What would she lie about, Mom?" He drew out the last word.

"Every . . . everything," she stuttered.

"I've always wanted to ask you a question." His voice was dead-like and calm. "What's the name of my first stuffed animal? You know, the one I carried with me as a child?"

# CHAPTER 27

"Just go! I know you're planning something. I'll hold her here." Archer had the con artist posing as his mother pinned in the kitchen.

"Mom. Get Dad and go through the escape route we talked about. You have ten minutes, twenty tops. Can you do it?" I asked.

"Yes, but, Ann, maybe . . . maybe . . . there's another way." Her eyes pleaded with mine.

"The Elders trained me for this. No one else can do it. I'm sorry, Mom." I rubbed her shoulder. "Promise me you'll get Dad and hurry, okay? If we take too long, the Jacks will notice we're gone and flee."

"Let me go!" Atarah screeched. "I love you more than any mother. Your real mom was a whiny, weak woman. She could never accomplish what I have. Think of our plans. We can rule the Jacks. Don't back out now. She'll destroy us!" Archer held her firmly against the counter.

I gave my mom one last squeeze.

"I'm honored to be your mother," she said with tears streaming down her cheeks.

"Please tell everyone I love them and I'm sorry." *Devon.* Could a heart actually break? My death would crush him.

"Ann!" Archer yelled.

I stopped at the door and turned.

"Is it a bomb?"

I didn't answer.

"It's okay, I knew this was a possibility."

I raised an eyebrow.

"My dad. I'd planned to stop you. But now . . . I'll stay here and make sure my—this Jack doesn't interfere. Tell everyone I'm sorry."

"Archer?"

"Yeah?"

"You have ten minutes." After all he'd done, I still couldn't let him die.

"I love you, Ann." His voice broke. "I'll stay here if I have to." He kept hold of his fake mother but bent over the counter like he was in extreme pain.

My eyes closed. He believed he was sacrificing his life to save mine. He didn't know my plan to detonate the bomb on site. My stomach sank but I continued.

Out of time. "Thank-you." I turned and ran.

Ten, twenty minutes max, was all I had to sprint to the furnace room where the Elders had placed the bomb. The first hallway I dashed down was clear. A large group of Jacks from England filled the second hallway. I'd noticed them before, stuck in their clique with their conversations about everything being 'bloody' this and 'bloody' that. They loitered in the hallway, clasping china cups filled with what I assumed was hot tea.

Great. I'd have to weave through each one like some bloody obstacle course. Another irony I wouldn't have time to think about.

Each access point caused me panic right before placing my hand on the pad. When the doors clicked open, I said a prayer of thanks.

I got to the last door and a familiar voice called, "Miss Baker. Wait!"

I froze, my back to the High Priest. The seconds ticked away.

"Yes?" I smoothed my hair and turned to face him. Showtime.

"You seem to be in a hurry. What's the rush?" His eyebrow lifted.

"Oh, you know. Wedding stuff." That's the best I could do? I tried to rebound. "I just had my dress fitting, and the hem is too long. I'm on my way to the laundry room to get some thread for the seamstress." Better. I was in the general area, so he might just buy it.

I had to get my breathing under control and manage to stop the perspiration from forming. The shaking from head to toe also needed to stop.

*There's something not right.* The High Priest was on to me.

"Atarah was looking for you. She said something about the lighting in the Hub. It's not bright enough." I kept my expression blank.

*When this is over, I'll make sure Atarah's death is slow and painful.* He frowned.

The chance I needed. "Okay, they're expecting me back. I'll see you at the ceremony." I turned and walked back to the door.

Please don't stop me.

"Ann."

I held my breath.

"Don't be late. She won't like it," he said.

I gave a respectful bow and went through the door and down the hall to the furnace room. Fool. He should have gone with his gut.

I had ten minutes.

Finding the locked box took seconds, exactly like our practice, but this time, I couldn't get it open because my hands were trembling. I shook to loosen them a few times and rolled my shoulders. My fingerprints were the only ones programmed to detonate the bomb, so I needed to keep them steady. After a few tries, I was able to push in the numbers for the combination and lift out the device. When I placed my finger on the detonation button, the explosion would be instantaneous.

I pictured Devon's face again, his grumpy scowl the first day we met on the beach. I smiled. His surprised look when I flattened him during the Kubotan lesson. I chuckled a little. And the kiss, our spectacular kiss. His love blazed so pure and deep, even thinking about it now took my breath away. Oh, but his soulful eyes that told me so much was what I'd remember the most. That's what I'd think of when pushing the detonation switch. That and the knowledge he'd be happy again.

A light radiated from within as peace and contentment washed through me, and I wasn't afraid anymore. I picked up the device, tilted my face up to the heavens, and smiled.

# CHAPTER 28

"**N**o!" Devon yelled.

The switch dropped from my hand onto the table.

"Devon?" Had I died already? Wait. We were still in the furnace room. "What are you doing here?"

"He's here to help us."

I swung around. Dread and disbelief at the sight of my mom and dad almost knocked me off my feet. "What are you doing? You're supposed to be off the compound by now."

"We're finishing what we started thousands of years ago. Our job has always been to protect you. We're not quitting now."

"Mom, you don't understand. I'm the only one who can detonate the bomb. I made a vow to the Elders."

She reached into a pocket and held up a pair of latex gloves. "Technology. Don't you love it? I lifted a print from one of your glasses. Your Dad is a Seer and a molecular scientist. He's quite handy." She patted him on the arm, and they shared a smile. "Anyway, we transferred your prints onto these gloves."

No way. "I can't let you."

"Ann." Devon held both my arms and pleaded, "For me?"

"I have to do this." Tears streamed down my face. "Don't you see? It was me the Elders asked. This is *my* destiny!" My insides were being torn apart. *Go with Devon* fought with my need to finish the mission. What if the gloves didn't work? What then? Now sobbing, I added, "The Seers knew this all along—that it would be me to save one of the groups. I don't mind the sacrifice, Devon. I promise. I can die knowing the Readers are safe and that you'll be happy again."

His tormented eyes connected with mine. A mistake—I couldn't look away. I grabbed him to me, blinded by emotion, and the need to feel him one more time took over.

"Ann." His lips met mine.

My hands twisted in his shirt while thousands of sparks fired through my blood, the love so intense, it about shattered my heart.

"I can't leave you here," he said.

I reached up and cupped his cheek. I needed a moment to look at him. So handsome, with eyes so dark and intense. It was more than that though. His beauty went right to his soul. One more kiss. I stood on tiptoes to reach his soft, full lips. His arms wrapped around me in desperation, his lips fused on mine, unrelenting. My mission became murky. I was losing myself. I couldn't leave him.

No. I pushed him away.

Devon's eyes met Mom's. He nodded. They had a plan?

"I love you, Ann. Please don't fight me on this."

"Wh . . . what do you—?"

He moved with lightning speed, lifting me off my feet, and slung me over his shoulder.

"Get her out now," my dad shouted.

"Wait." I squirmed and struggled. "Let me go."

"They've made their choice, Ann. And it's you they want to save."

"I won't let them!" I tried to kick and hit myself free, but he held on like a vise.

"I love you, Ann." Mom had already put on the gloves.

"I'll love you forever, Sweet Pea," Dad joined in.

I remembered the pet name he had for me in a surge of warm love. *Oh, Dad.* "Dad. I remember Sweet Pea." I struggled. I'd get free somehow and save my parents.

His eyes misted. "That's exactly what we hoped for. You'll remember us clearly soon. When you do, you'll understand this better. Your mom and I love you very much."

"I love you, too. Both of you. Please don't do this." Sobs racked through me.

"Time to go." Devon swung back to the exit. Before we left, he told my parents, "I'll take good care of her; I promise."

Using my hands to press against Devon's back, I lifted my head to see them one last time. "Mom, Dad." Tears clouded my vision, but my parents' smiles came through.

They held hands, and Mom said, "We know you will, Devon. Thank you. It's time now."

Devon still had me over his shoulder and began the run down a darkened hallway, out of the compound. The furnace room was right by an exit, so it wasn't far. "Please don't make any noise. If anyone hears us, we won't make it out."

I had accepted my death, but Devon needed to live and love again. So I remained quiet.

Once we were in the Jeep outside the compound gate, Devon's shoulders seemed to relax.

In one quick move, I had the glovebox open, handcuffs connecting Devon's wrist to the steering wheel, and the key out of the ignition.

"I hope you'll understand why I have to do this."

Devon's eyes doubled in size, and he shouted, "No. Ann. No!" He struggled against the restraints, swearing and pulling at them.

I stepped out of the Jeep. "I'm so sorry."

"There's no time to save your parents!" He pounded his free hand against the steering wheel.

"Please forgive me . . ." I couldn't continue.

He struggled with the handcuffs. After a few moments, his body sagged, and his head rested on the steering wheel. "I forgive you." His head came up and his eyes met mine. "What you're doing right now is exactly why I love you so much. But listen to me. I can live without anything else on this planet. But not you. Don't do it, Ann. Don't make me live without you."

"Remember my vision? You'll be happy again. It's the only way I can do this. I love you so much."

I allowed myself one last look before I turned and ran with every ounce of energy left in my body. I had to stop my parents, even if it meant knocking them out and dragging them to safety.

I entered the compound again from the back exit. The lights were off, so I used the walls as my guide. Hurry. I had only seconds. I rounded the last corner and ran right into a large body. An arm gripped me, a cloth with a sickly, chemical smell clamped over my face and nose.

The world faded and disappeared.

# CHAPTER 29

## DEVON

*TWO YEARS LATER*

"I KNOW THIS IS a hard day for you," Lucy said, eyeing me. "A hard day for all of us."

Every year, on the anniversary of the extinction of the Jacks, we'd booked the same cabin at Cannon Beach, our favorite place in the world. It sat fifty steps up from the sand, but it was well worth the hike up and down. I could heal here under the starlit skies

"I'm okay." I gave her shoulder a shove. "Go hover over someone else." I smiled so she'd know I was only kidding. We sat on the sand, alone for the first time in days.

"It's nice to get a little breather from the kids, pets, and spouses, isn't it?"

"Yes, although it gives me time to think about it, you

know?" I closed my eyes to hear the sights and sounds of the ocean. The crashing of the waves calmed me. The salty smells, kids playing and laughing, gave me hope.

"It's a tough day, but a lot of good things happened when the Jacks died." She put her head on my shoulder.

I nodded, because I couldn't speak. I hadn't been able to save them.

"We've been able to rebuild our lives." She glanced back toward the cabin.

"Yes, the sacrifice was huge. Have you seen the statue they've built? They plan to place it in the entry of our new compound." Just like Ann's vision had predicted, the bomb had destroyed Samara, exploding it into tiny fragments. The new site was nearby, in Verlot, Washington, another small town that sat at the foot of a large mountain.

"Adam told me. Have you been there lately? It looks great." Lucy's eyes lit up.

"I visited last week. I'm glad we decided to keep our identity from the world a bit longer. I don't think they're quite ready for us." I smiled.

"The world is healing though. The crime rate has already decreased by fifty percent, the restructured United Nations is stronger and has implemented new peace programs, the extreme religious cults have nearly disappeared. Who knew the Jacks controlled most of those? All of this in only two years," Lucy said all at once, running out of breath toward the end. Yeah, my sister, the dreamer. I was glad to see some of them come true.

"So, Adam, huh?" I asked.

"Now, don't go teasing me. He was obnoxious in the 1920s, but he's really changed." She smiled and dug her feet into the sand.

"I guess having to wait a hundred years for a proper kiss will do that to a guy."

"He said I was worth waiting for." She giggled, then became serious. "Do you ever wonder what your life would be like if things went differently on that day?"

"Every day. I think about it all the time."

"What do you think about all the time?" My wife joined us and sat on my lap, putting her arms around my neck. "Hi, Lucy," she said and smiled.

Lucy jumped and brushed the sand from her jeans. "Now that you're here, I'm going to try to steal some time with my nephew. You two hog him all the time."

I wanted to talk to Lucy a little more, but neither of us had figured out a way to discuss that day two years ago. Whenever the subject arose, we'd try to change it. My new wife had all sorts of questions, but she sensed it wasn't a subject Lucy and I wanted to rehash. Maybe in time. Perhaps I would talk to her a little more once the guilt subsided. The beach had me in a mellow mood, perhaps I could speak about my failure on this trip. "We'll be back in a few minutes to take over Henry duty," I told Lucy's retreating back.

"Sure thing. I'll see you two later." She trotted off toward the house we'd rented.

"I thought she'd never leave." I wrapped my arms around my love and flipped her over onto her back. She giggled as I leaned down and kissed her sweet, full lips, leaving us both breathless.

"I love you so much." Her hands ran through my hair as tears escaped her eyes.

I wiped them and kissed her again. "Don't be sad."

"I can't help it. They gave up their lives for all of us. I have you, and now we have Henry. I'm sad and happy at the same time. It's confusing."

My lips brushed against hers again. It never got old. The love I had for her filled every molecule in my body, making me almost burst from it.

She pulled me closer. "Wow. The tingles keep getting stronger and stronger. If it keeps going like this, every time you kiss me, I'll faint or something. That'd be embarrassing." She laughed.

She stopped and gazed into my eyes.

I said, "I didn't think it was possible, but I love you more every day." I ran my fingers through her soft hair.

"Me, too."

I kissed her again. Even better.

"Break it up, you two. Henry's hungry, and he won't take the bottle from me." Lucy was back interrupting the moment. But I didn't mind, because she brought our beautiful son. I considered ignoring them for another moment to get another quick kiss, but a loud gurgle snapped me from my plan. Three months old, and he had to be the happiest child on earth. His eyes sparkled with innocent joy. Or was it because we were so happy? I glanced at my wife again, her smile even more beautiful.

I sat up, and Lucy plopped Henry in my arms. "I'll start the barbecue. Dinner should be ready in about twenty minutes." She headed back up toward the cabin.

Henry still squirmed a little, so I stood to rock him. The sun sat low on the horizon, and the sky had taken on its nightly show of blended colors before sunset. I swayed back and forth with Henry, kissing him before I sang in his ear.

"This is it," Ann gasped.

"What's the matter?" I asked.

"This was my vision. Remember? I saw you with a baby by the ocean. I didn't see myself because I was doing the watching." Ann laughed. "I guess I should have figured that out."

"Was that the same vision you talked about right before you almost pushed the detonation button?"

"Yes." She reached over and caressed Henry's soft hair. "Right before you and my parents came in."

"After the Elders told me their plan, I knew there'd be no stopping you, my brave warrior." I held Henry in my right arm and embraced Ann with my left. I kissed each one on their cheek, lingering a little longer on Ann's.

Her eyes softened and she asked in hopeful voice. "You ready to talk about it a little?"

I nodded, but was unsure if I could go *there*.

"I know this is what my parents wanted, but sometimes I feel guilty."

I took a deep breath and forced myself to talk. "I feel the same. I keep replaying those last few moments, trying to figure out if there was a way to save both you and your parents, but I come up empty every time. There's nothing we could've done." The guilt lifted a little. Maybe talking about it would be a good thing.

"I still can't believe she had my fingerprints duplicated."

"She was smart, like her daughter."

"And my dad. He wouldn't leave her." She closed her eyes. "I understand it. I wouldn't want to live without you either."

"You'll never have to." I squeezed her shoulder.

"I guess we have Archer to thank, as well," she said.

"Yeah. I'm still shocked when I think about his deceit and betrayal. Sure, he pulled through at the end by stopping Atarah. But he would've spent his life in prison for killing Markus. Sometimes I think it's better that he died."

"You're right. I couldn't imagine him behind bars. I'm still conflicted about Archer though. I can't help but think that Atarah was somehow able to influence his thoughts. Do you think it's possible?"

"Perhaps." I wished for an hour with him. After I beat him to a pulp, I'd make him answer all my questions.

She stared at the ocean for a long moment. "Do you think it could've been Archer who dragged me to safety? If so, he might be alive."

"I don't think so. It goes against his character to remain silent. I would think he'd try to reconnect somehow." Archer was never one to sit back. My hands curled into fists thinking about it.

Ann took my clenched hand, kissed it, and placed it against her cheek. My anger and frustration evaporated, and a flood of love and contentment filled my soul.

*How does she do that? Calm me when no one else can?*

She giggled. "Because we're Soul Mates, that's why."

"My thoughts are still coming through?"

"Just the strong ones." She quit laughing and placed her hand on my cheek. "I feel the same."

We stood for a quiet moment with our hands linked. I smiled and leaned down to kiss her as the sun relaxed its hold on the painted sky. Another spectacular day. And I knew tomorrow would be even better.

The man observed the young family from a bench set off behind some beach scrub. He enjoyed the ocean and would often come just to listen to the waves hit the shore. A pretty, young woman, around nineteen years old, came and sat next to him. Her cheeks turned pink as she spoke.

"They're a beautiful family."

"Yes. I like to people watch. It can be entertaining," he said.

"Do you know them?" she asked.

"I knew a girl like her a long time ago. I loved her deeply, but I made mistakes and I couldn't fix them."

"That's too bad," the girl said.

They watched the family play in the surf for a few minutes.

"Did you ever try to make things right?" she asked

"I sacrificed my happiness for hers. Painful, but worth it. I saved her life, but it was she who really saved mine."

"Oh, that's so romantic." The girl placed her hand over her heart.

*Mortals,* the man thought. They're so simplistic.

The man had never considered it romantic, because he had lost her, the woman he loved. A pulsing ache ripped through him.

"Will you ever see her again?"

"No," he said.

The man had learned to lie with the best, and today was no different.

## THE END

# ACKNOWLEDGEMENTS

I LOVE MY BETA READERS! When I wrote my first book, I didn't even know about beta readers. There are people who would take time out of their busy schedule to give help and feedback? And for free?! Yes, in my book there isn't a better person on the planet! (Pun intended) I couldn't have done it without all of you! Dana Mason, Emily Mettner, Karen Harper, Francis Vanessa Valladares Duarte, Jennifer Trevino, Rosie Amber, Sherry Christenson, Heather Taylor, Audrey Rich, Kelly Lovatt, Maari Hammond (Maari Loves Her Indies) Nancy Thompson, Amy McGlone Colorado Marshal, Rebecca Goss, Melesia Tully, Tamara Graham, Jacinda Mumbi, Jan Hinds, Char Webster, Linda Moffitt, Kathryn Gates-Gustafson, Daniel Randall

NANCY SALING THOMPSON: You did double duty for this one—and I couldn't appreciate you more! Your suggestions were spot on as usual. Thanks for your expertise and friendship. You are the best!

JULIE HARTNETT: Just because. (You are also the best!)

Amy McGlone (Rebels and Readers Book Blog) You are a GREAT beta reader. I don't think I would publish without your feedback!

Dana Mason: You have quickly become my go-to beta for all the intricate plot issues, character development—well, everything. Your eye for detail is unsurpassed!

Donna Feyen (More Than a Review): Even though you don't usually read YA—you made an exception for The Reader. I really appreciate your support and kind words.

Maari Hammond—I love your kind spirit and enthusiasm. You make writing fun!

Kendra (Lola Kay) Sikorski—You have been with me since the beginning. Every author should have a Kendra! You are priceless. Thanks so much for all your help—words cannot express.

To my editors: Nancy Saling Thompson (Author and Editor) and Karen Harper (Purple Orchid Editing)

Victorine Leiske (Blue Valley Author Services)—Thank you for the beautiful cover. I love it ☺

Sister Laurel, Laurie or Elore (Depending on the mood) We WILL move to Scotland and sit outside and read and write and . . . well, you know the rest.

Last, but certainly not least, MY FAMILY. You know who you are ☺